Pop

Merry Xmas

Di + Carl

23

OUTLAW'S CODE

**Center Point
Large Print**

**This Large Print Book carries the
Seal of Approval of N.A.V.H.**

OUTLAW'S CODE

Max Brand®

CENTER POINT PUBLISHING
THORNDIKE, MAINE

This Center Point Large Print edition
is published in the year 2007 by arrangement with
Golden West Literary Agency.

ISBN-10: 1-60285-056-9
ISBN-13: 978-1-60285-056-9

Library of Congress Cataloging-in-Publication Data

Brand, Max, 1892-1944.
    Outlaw's code / Max Brand.--Center Point large print ed.
        p. cm.
    ISBN-13: 978-1-60285-056-9 (lib. bdg. : alk. paper)
    1. Outlaws--Fiction. 2. Large type books. I. Title.

PS3511.A87O98 2007
813'.52--dc22

2007017743

OUTLAW'S CODE

1

Marshal Neilan had slept eight hours a night for two weeks. He had eaten three square meals, and had a full hour's siesta after each lunch, and yet the marshal was tired. He looked tired, and he was tired. He had a battered face and he had a battered soul. He was mortally weary, and his weariness came from walking constantly in danger of his life.

They were all out for the marshal. The drug runners, and the smugglers of Chinese across the border; the yeggs and thugs of the river towns; the horse thieves and the cattle rustlers; and all those clever internationalists who occasionally drifted in the direction of El Paso and points east and west of that cheerful city; all of these and many odd types had it in for the marshal.

He was tireless, he was unforgetting, he was unforgiving, and he was incorruptible.

Men said that Steve Malley, the great smuggler, once laid a stack of a thousand hundred-dollar bills on the marshal's desk and got it back the next day. After that, they gave up trying to bribe him. But everyone wondered why he kept on at the job. Certainly it was not the money involved. His salary was beggarly small; if he wanted to turn back to his law office, he could make ten times as much with the greatest ease. Neither did he enjoy great fame; he was rarely in the papers.

In fact, what kept the marshal at his post was an

odd thing—a sense of duty so pure and noble that his labors rewarded themselves. But still he could be tired, and he was especially weary this morning, as he wrote on a slip of paper: "Dear Bill, Will you send Lawrence Grey over to my office?"

He dispatched this note by his office boy.

Then he turned and looked out across the roofs, and listened to the murmur and the rumblings of the city, until the sound took on another character and seemed to him like the drumming sound of bees in the sunshine, and the still, ominous purring of the mosquitoes in the river flats. He looked at the yellow sands of the desert beyond the town, and the rock faces of the hills that made his horizon. That was where he wanted to be—anywhere out there, in the open. But his work was too great and spread over too wide a field. Electricity had to carry his thoughts, and this was the center of power. He had to sit here in the center and send out emissaries to spin the farther margins of his web.

He was in the midst of these melancholy thoughts when his office boy returned and opened the door for an excited man who came with him, Deputy Sheriff Sam Tucker, late of Tucson, and other points west where trouble was in the air.

Sam Tucker said, " 'Lo, Marshal Neilan. Look a' here, Marshal, is it a joke?"

The marshal, by painful degrees, dragged his thoughts back from the great open places and turned his tired, battered face toward the other.

"Is what a joke, Sam?" said he.

"You wrote a note over. You sent it over, and you says that you wanta see Rinky Dink. Is that right, or is it a joke?"

"It's not a joke," said the marshal. "How many people know that you've got young Lawrence Grey?"

Sam Tucker looked uneasily over his shoulder toward the door. He looked toward the ceiling, and he looked also toward the floor. It seemed that he suspected everything around. Then he stepped closer and laid a brown hand on the edge of the marshal's desk.

"Not a damn soul," he whispered. "And thank God for it! Nobody knows, and nobody's gonna know till we have to let it out. That'll be time. The fool newspapers, they'll blow the word around. They'll be shoutin' out loud, and his friends will hear. It'll be harder and worse to hold him then, than it is to hold freezin' nitroglycerine. And—"

"How did you get Grey?" asked the marshal, curiously.

"Didn't the chief tell you?"

"No. I haven't heard. You fellows have been very close-mouthed."

"Smythe and Ridgeby and Allen and Fulton and Meggs, they went out. They all went out to make the plant," said the deputy sheriff.

"About the five best men you have," suggested the marshal.

"Not about; they *are* the best," said Sam Tucker.

9

"They're clean and away the best. Who else would we be sending for Don Diablo?"

"I suppose so," said the marshal. "And what happened?"

"Well, they got a good start. The Mexicans had framed him," said Sam Tucker. "They took most of the punching, too."

"How bad was it?" said the marshal.

"A couple of Mexicans will never eat frijoles any more," said Sam Tucker, carelessly. "Meggs is in a pretty bad way, but they say he'll pull through. Smythe and Allen, they're laid up, but they'll be reporting back for duty in about a month, I guess. The whole bunch was lucky, any way you take it."

The marshal half closed his eyes and seemed to be dreaming.

"Yes," he said, "they were a lucky lot."

"About that note, now," said Sam Tucker, with a forced laugh. "The chief, he just wanted me to drop over and find out what the joke was."

"There's no joke," said the marshal. "I want to see him. I want to see him here."

The jaw of the deputy sheriff dropped.

"You don't mind if I ask again, sir," said he. "It's Rinky Dink that you mean, all right? It's Don Diablo, is it?"

"Yes," said the marshal. "It's Lawrence Grey. Tell your chief that I have to have him here. And your chief along with him, if that's possible."

Sam Tucker left. He slid through the door with an

alarmed glance behind him, as though he were departing by the skin of his teeth from the presence of a madman.

And the marshal turned back in his chair and continued to stare out the window, blankly, sadly, for nearly an hour.

In the meantime, there were many calls on his telephone, and many taps at his door. But he refused everyone. He was saving himself. He was too tired a man for more than one interview such as he intended to have that morning.

Eventually they came.

First, two guards came through the doorway. Each wore revolvers; each carried a sawed-off shotgun. They entered, stepped half a pace to either side of the door, and faced inwards, holding their shotguns at the ready.

Behind them appeared the sheriff, who came in, nodded briefly at the marshal, and, taking up his position in the center of the room, faced the door in his turn. He allowed no weapons to be visible, but the bulges under his coat were not made by packages of candy.

When these preparations had been made, two more men appeared, assisting between them, as it seemed, a third, whose wrists were held together by heavy irons, connecting through a powerful double chain with other manacles that fitted over the ankles.

He was bundled through the doorway.

The door was then closed, and the key turned in the lock.

"Well, Neilan," said the sheriff. "Here he is. I've known you close onto twenty years, Neilan—and so I've brought him when you called."

He was panting. He took out a handkerchief and wiped his forehead. But the movement was furtive, and his eyes never left the face of the prisoner.

The guards looked only at the man in chains, and so did the marshal. Yet Lawrence Grey was no abysmal brute in face or body. He was a slenderly made youth who might have been twenty-one when he smiled, and twenty-five when he was serious. But generally he was smiling. He had one of those pink and white complexions which refuses to be tanned by the fiercest sun; it merely becomes pinker—and whiter. His blond hair, to be sure, seemed rather sun-faded at the outer margin.

Lawrence Grey was dressed in neat flannels, and he wore a white shirt with a soft collar, and black tie of silk tied in a big flowing knot, such as Bohemians and artists are so fond of affecting. He wore a jaunty slouch hat, with the brim turned up on one side. And in general his appearance was that of a pleasant, casual young man. In New York he would never have drawn a second glance. For El Paso, he was just a trifle precious in his make-up.

"Thank you for bringing him," said the marshal. "You might introduce me to him, though."

"As if this hombre didn't know you," growled the sheriff. "But you tell him, Rinky Dink. You tell him if you know him."

"Of course I know Marshal Neilan," said Lawrence Grey.

And he smiled at the marshal, as if to say that he was honored to meet him, and that he was also, perhaps, honoring the marshal just a little.

In fact, he seemed a modest young man, and yet he gave a second impression of being rather sure of himself, in a quiet way. Young Englishmen often give the same effect.

"And I know you, Grey," said the marshal, "although this is the first time I've seen you. One hears about one another."

"Yes," said Grey, with another of his charming smiles. "One does."

"Listen at him talk," said the sheriff, half grinning and half snarling. "Sweet, ain't he? Look at him, Neilan. Butter'd melt in *his* mouth, all right."

"You don't need to point him out," said the marshal. "Now that you've brought him here, I want to ask another favor of you, old fellow."

"Go on," said the sheriff. "You know the sky is the limit, between you and me—only, don't spring another like this one!"

"I want you to send your strong boys back home, and I want you to go and sit in the outer office, yonder, and leave Grey in here alone with me."

The sheriff started to speak, and then stared. But he stared at the prisoner, not at the sheriff. He still looked at Grey as he answered:

"Leave you alone with Rinky Dink? You're crazy,

Neilan. You know you're crazy to ask that!"

"I'm asking just that," said the marshal. "He's loaded down with iron and I'm well armed, you know."

The sheriff shook his head, as a man does when he cannot offer a logical objection, though he feels resistant still.

"I don't like it. Fact is," he said, "I hate the idea of it!"

"I want to be alone with him," said the marshal, quietly.

At last the sheriff looked at him.

"You're never wrong, old son," he said at last. "And I hope to God that you're right now. I'll be sitting out there on springs. Make it as short as you can!"

2

The sheriff and the rest of his men had withdrawn from the office, with the exception of the second of the two bearers of the riot guns, and this worthy fellow, with a sour look at young Lawrence Grey and a wondering one at the marshal, now blurted out: "I don't wanta be botherin' you, sir, but suppose that I was just to stand here in a handy corner with this here gun, it might be tolerable useful."

The marshal nodded seriously at him.

"Thank you, Jerry," said he. "It's fellows like you that make life easier for us. But I'll have to trust myself alone with our young friend."

So the guard went out, shaking his head and closing the door slowly behind him, with a long, long look of doubt cast toward Lawrence Grey.

When he was gone, and the door at last closed, Neilan pointed to a chair.

"Sit down, Grey," said he. "Make yourself at home while I open the window."

He spent only a moment, loosening the catch which held the window down, and then lifted it with some effort, for it was a trifle wedged at either side.

When he turned around from his work, he found that Rinky Dink was sitting with the shackles and the double chain piled neatly beside his chair, his knees crossed, and his hands locked lightly across one of them.

The sheriff, looking at him without surprise, merely said, "Don't you want a smoke, Rinky?"

"I'd like one," said the boy, gratefully. "They're rather careless about the details over there in the jail."

"Here's Bull Durham and wheat straw papers," said the sheriff, taking them from a pocket. "But hold on. You have a fancy for Turkish blends, I think."

He opened a drawer of his desk and took out a package.

"Here's a sample parcel of Turkish stuff sent over the border for a small, select American manufacturer. But it got to the wrong address, Rinky, the way things will. Want to try it?"

"Of course," said Grey.

He made his cigarette with the leisurely speed of

15

one whose fingers need no watching; they guided themselves and solved their own problems.

The marshal made his own cigarette of Bull Durham. He lighted both smokes from one match, and afterwards tossed it onto the pile of steel shackles and tool-proof chain.

"That was rather a fast bit of work, wasn't it, Rinky?" he asked.

Lawrence Grey tilted a little in his chair and regarded the gleaming heap.

"The locks are rather old-fashioned," he said. "No, that wasn't a very fast job."

"A very neat one, though," said the marshal. "And I heard nothing. You must have wrapped the links with flannel."

"More or less," nodded Rinky. "I just held the chain between my legs."

"So there's no mystery at all," remarked Neilan, going back to the chair behind his desk.

"Oh, none at all," said the boy. "This is grand tobacco," he added. "Some day I want to get over to the section of the world where they grow this stuff."

"Well, you'll get there one day," answered Neilan.

"Not if the sheriff has his way," said Grey.

The marshal smiled, very faintly, and his battered face seemed suddenly younger.

"Why did you let them keep you a whole day?" he asked.

"Why? Oh, the jail has very strong bars. Toolproof and all that," answered the youngster.

"But it has to depend on locks," remarked Neilan.

"Very complicated new ones," said Grey.

The marshal shrugged his shoulders, apparently not convinced.

"I suppose that you wanted a rest," he suggested.

"Don't underrate the sheriff," warned Grey. "He's a formidable fellow. Every honest man is dangerous to people like me, you know!"

And he opened his eyes and nodded. He looked like a child, for the moment.

"I don't underrate the sheriff," said Neilan. "But something tells me that you're not likely to end your career in this town. It will have to be in a much bigger place than this, Rinky. By the way, who gave you that new name the sheriff is so fond of using? Who called you Don Diablo?"

The boy sighed.

"You know how it is," he said confidingly. "If someone has a bit of bad luck, let's say, and takes quite a fall, he's apt to call the other fellow the devil. It was only that."

"Well, Grey," said the marshal, "or Rinky Dink, or Don Diablo—I'm glad to have you here under any or all of those names. I've been waiting for years to see you face to face."

"Thank you," said the boy. "You'll understand if I cannot say that I've been hoping for the same thing?"

The marshal chuckled.

"Now I'll tell you why I've sent for you, Rinky," said he. "I have on hand just the job for you—the very thing that's made to order for you."

A shadow came over Grey's eyes, a mere suggestion of disappointment and disgust.

"Well?" he said slowly.

But the marshal had read the meaning of that passing shadow and he said: "It's not a graft, Rinky. It's not likely that you could make much money out of it. It's merely a good chance for you to go and break your young neck."

Lawrence Grey regarded him earnestly. He drew in a breath of smoke; he touched his throat with femininely sensitive fingers.

"Yes?" said he.

"Here's the rest of that tobacco," replied Neilan. "You smoke away at that while I talk. I'll begin by reading you a letter that I got four years ago: it runs like this."

He spread a paper on the desk and read:

Dear Marshal Neilan,

You · may remember me from the old Brownsville days. The boys called me "Brick" then. It may help you to identify me if you recall the fellow who was accused of stealing Jay Saunders' bay gelding. I was the Brick Forbes of that episode.

Yes, I stepped a little too high and touched the ground not often enough, in those days. Since then I've turned respectable. And I want to tell you the cause of it.

I was down in old Mexico at San Vicente. It was running high, wide and handsome in those days. I understand that it still is. I had washed out some gold in the hills behind the town, and I came down to Vicente to have a bust.

I had it, all right. Before I finished, I'd spent my money and got into a fight. Two Mexicans had me cornered and they were about to let the light into me when a fellow came by and slammed one of them over the head with the barrel of his six-shooter, and kicked the second one into the street.

This stranger who rescued me was around middle age, about five feet nine or ten in height, and the peculiar point in his appearance was a divided beard. It split in the center and parted outwards, and ended in two points. He had dark eyes. His beard was gray. That's all the description I can give him, except that he was well dressed.

He took me by the shoulders and brought me out into the light.

He said: "I've been watching you. You've played the fool, but you're not as much of a fool as you pretend to be. This nonsense doesn't amuse you. Go home and be a good boy. This will take you back to the states."

He dropped a whole wallet into my pocket, and afterwards I counted a shade over a thousand dollars in it. I sat down with that money and had a think. I saw that the stranger was right. I had been chasing a good time all over the West, but I never had found it. I had blown my pay every month, but I always damned myself on Monday morning. I was sick of the life, and I hadn't known it. I had been at the door of the jail twenty times, and all for nothing. So I decided to pull out.

First, I asked for the name of my benefactor, and I was told that he was called John Ray. He was a high stepper, and a great spender, and everybody's friend in San Vicente. I tried to see him and thank him and tell him that I was going to follow his good advice, but he was out of town.

So I packed up and left San Vicente and went back to Pennsylvania. I had been raised in the country there, and I went right back to the old ground and sank the rest of my thousand after railroad fare was subtracted in buying some of the worst land in the world, at less than twenty dollars an acre. I got about fifty acres for what I thought a bargain, but I found out that it was the worst ground in the world. It was covered with outcropping soft black stone, and about one sheep to three acres was enough to keep the grass cropped short.

I couldn't live on that fool place. I went to work in the town as a carpenter and kept at that for nearly five years. Then, all at once, along came a fellow with a pink face and a foxy eye and wanted to buy my land. He offered me my original price. But I held on for more. He came up with a thousand, and finally I upped him to three thousand cash. When I had that offer from him, I simply told him to go to the devil. The land wasn't worth that much on the face of it and it never would be. I decided that I would find out what was under the face of it.

Well, when I learned that that fellow was a coal miner, it gave me my lead. You won't believe it; the outcropping on that wretched land was coal. I'd bought fifty acres of as good anthracite as a body could find in the world! And that was in Pennsylvania, where even the worst old fools and the smallest kids know all about coal! And I had spent five years cursing my black rocks!

That made me rich. I didn't have to use any intelligence. I simply sat by and let a company work the mine and took a big fat percentage for myself. I got so much money that I could afford to sit back and just pick up the good things that offered themselves, here and there. So I've stacked money on top of money for ten years and lived the softest sort of a life. I have somewhere between five and six millions today.

Now comes the rub. I get a dizzy spell one day. "Indigestion!" say I.

"Hardening of the arteries," says the doctor.

"What does that mean?" I ask.

"Make your will. I'll explain later," says he.

I go to make my will, and there's another rub. I've been raising money, not a family. I have no wife or children. The nearest relations are a batch of second cousins, as hard as steel and as small as conies. The tightest, meanest lot of people I ever knew. If I pass out tomorrow, they get my whole fortune, and split it into fifty parcels—just enough to make them all mean *and* self-satisfied, the rest of their days.

Then I look at the charities. But what the devil do I care about charities? What did charities ever do for me? No, I want to give my cash to a human being. But, mind you, all I've made in the past fifteen years have been business acquaintances. You can't call them friends.

Now I come to the point where I appeal to you. I think back to the old Western days. Those were the times when I found people that I loved around me. But they were a harum-scarum lot. Pretty worthless a lot of them were—as worthless as I was myself. Only one man ever really did me any good. He gave me hard cash; he gave me good advice; and with his money I'd bought my fortune so to speak.

I remembered John Ray of San Vicente.

Considering the pace he was going when I last saw him or heard of him in San Vicente, he was probably dead long years since. A man can't be the friend of everyone in town very long. It spoils the digestion first and empties the pocketbook second. But if John Ray is dead, at least he may have left some descendants, sons or daughters.

The moment I think of that, I get a flash of inspiration. I feel pretty good inside and out. And straight away, I send a registered letter to San Vicente, addressed to John Ray.

I'm not surprised when it comes back, the addressee not having been found. And next I send down a special messenger all the way to San Vicente. A good, solid fellow I can trust. A fellow with a pair of hands and a head, too. He goes down to San Vicente. I get a wire from him saying that he thinks he's on the trail. And the next thing I know, there's a small item in a Pittsburgh paper referring to the death of my man down there in San Vicente. His body has been found in the lake among the lily pads. He must have drunk too much tequila and fallen into the water; there's no signs of foul play.

That's very good. But Sam Bowman never tasted a drop in his life and never made a misstep. He was straighter and more careful than a certified accountant. So I send down a private detective named Richard Burton. I wait three months and never hear a word from him.

After that, I say to myself: Something's rotten in the state of Denmark. Those two men have been bumped off because I sent them looking for John Ray.

And here's the point where you enter, Neilan. If I can't get men from back here to locate John Ray in San Vicente, you can. I'll pay five times any reasonable fee. John Ray or one of his blood is what I want to find. I pass along the job to you. Whatever money you have to spend on the job is all right with me. I'll send you the checks for it.

Only, for God's sake, work fast. According to the infernal doctors, I'm walking a tightrope that's likely to break under me any minute. And if I fall too soon, six millions will tumble into the hands of about fifty hard-fisted, miserly, mean-souled scoundrels, all because there happens to be a slight taint of their blood in me.

3

At this point the marshal paused in his reading.

"That was four years ago," said he. "There's two things worth noting down. One is that John Ray hasn't been located. The other is that Brick Forbes is still hanging onto his life out yonder in Pittsburgh. At the last report, he had been living on graham crackers and water, or some such diet, for three years. And now they've put him to bed and only give him the air for an hour a day in a wheel chair that they take over the bumps with special care.

"But still Brick Forbes is fighting like a Trojan, and he won't leave off fighting until the last breath is out of his body. He doesn't want his money to go into

24

the hands of his relatives. They're a little too distant to suit him, and they're too unlike the type of man he respects. They've never been west to thaw out; they've never learned to spread their elbows at the board."

"How many men have you sent to San Vicente?" asked the boy.

"I've sent three, in the four years. The first fellow got tired of the job and came back, having accomplished nothing. The second was a sound man, and he stayed down there for months, using up my money and faking reports to me. Then I learned that he was too canny to be honest. He'd been prospecting on the side, he struck it rich, and finally he threw up the job and stuck to his mining claim.

"These fellows, between them, had used up two years. And poor Forbes was sending me pathetic letters from Pittsburgh. He was getting worse and worse.

"So I picked out one of the best men I had. Perhaps, you know him. H. J. Broom."

"I know Dolly Broom," said the boy. "We met one evening in the Big Bend."

"The Big Bend is quite a place to meet in," observed the marshal, with a wrinkling about his eyes.

"Well," said the boy, with a similar smile, "that evening we both needed plenty of room. But Dolly was all right. I liked him—outside of his profession. What happened to him when he went to San Vicente?"

The marshal paused and shook his head.

"Broom worked for well over a year and got nothing. But at the end of that time, I had a short note from him saying that he was on the right trail, and that it would prove to be a surprising one. Then all communications from him stopped. I thought nothing for a month or more. He might be working out the last details in silence. But then his continued silence began to worry me. So I sent down to investigate Broom's silence. To put the report briefly, he had been seen and known in and about San Vicente, but some time before he had disappeared.

"From that day to this, I've been looking for the right man to send to San Vicente. And at last I've found him."

Lawrence Grey looked at the marshal in candid astonishment.

"You're not serious, marshal, are you?" he asked.

"Of course I am," said Neilan.

The other shook his head.

"Tell me why I should do it?" asked Grey.

"For the simplest reason in the world. Three people have already died or disappeared on the trail. So the job is made to order for you."

Lawrence Grey said nothing for a moment, and finally he leaned a little forward and eyed the marshal with eyes as straight as ruled lines.

"I don't make it out," said he.

"You do, though," said Neilan. "Already every muscle of you is twitching to be off to San Vicente. Confess that I'm right."

Then he added: "Don't pretend that you're a dyed-in-the-wool criminal, Rinky Dink. I've watched your career. It's been a bright one. But you've been in the game for the fun you get out of it! Come, come! Tell the truth, confess. I won't repeat it."

The boy sat back in his chair.

He said: "Well, what am I to do? Break jail and ride south?"

The marshal smiled.

"You won't have to break jail," said he. "Wait a moment."

He called in the sheriff, and the sheriff came with a hand beneath his coat. When he saw Don Diablo unshackled, his hand flashed out with a gun in it.

"Now, steady up," said the marshal. "I've brought you in to ask for a two months' parole for this boy."

"Parole?" said the sheriff. "Neilan, say that again! Parole for a murderer?"

"Stuff," said the marshal. "You mean the two Mexicans? You know about them, I suppose?"

"I know they're dead," said the sheriff.

"Dead on the other side of the border, for one thing. For another, one of them was Francisco Vittorio; the other was Juan Cappano. And Old Mexico offers a price for either of 'em, dead or alive. As for your own agents, tell me what the devil they meant by making an arrest on the other side of the river?"

The sheriff blinked at this startling array of facts.

"Neilan," he mourned, "it was right on the edge of the river. The lights from the house made a path right across to our side. There'll never be a state complaint about that arrest. Mexico doesn't care who catches Don Diablo, so long as he's caught!"

"I care, though," replied the marshal. "You go ahead and arrange the parole, like a good fellow. Or else, just turn your head at the jail. That's the better way. Let the boy take care of himself. Is that agreeable to you, Rinky?"

"That's all right," said Grey.

"Who unlocked the irons?" asked the sheriff, angrily. "Did you take it on yourself to do that, Neilan?"

"Come here to the window a moment," said the marshal. "Grey, you might as well get ready to leave, if you don't mind."

He drew the sheriff to the window, and there he said to him quietly: "Don't be a fool, old son. The boy can land you in all sorts of hot water because of the place you arrested him. I know that it's been done before. I know there's such a thing as railroading fellows who deserve it. But this is an exceptional case. Grey has too many brains."

The sheriff groaned.

"Well, then—" he began.

Turning back toward the prisoner, he was amazed to see him sitting once more invested in the full weight of the manacles and chains.

He strode to the boy and tried the irons on wrists and ankles. Both were securely locked.

Then he stepped back with a scowl.

"I don't understand any of it, Neilan," he said. "All I know is that it's a bad business. I don't understand it and I don't like it."

He called loudly, and his four men rushed in eagerly, like a dog pack expecting to be fed.

"Take him back!" commanded the sheriff.

And leaving last of all, he glowered over his shoulder at the marshal, and shook a solemn head.

4

When Rinky Dink, alias Lawrence Grey, alias Don Diablo, found himself at last inside the jail, he carried with him from the office of the marshal the remainder of that pound of curiously good blended Turkish tobaccos, good as only a sample can be. It was put away in his pocket. He carried also the memory of something which was almost a promise.

On the way, he considered it. It was not exactly a promise, either. It was something more and something less. He had not given his word to the marshal, and neither had the marshal striven with threats to induce him.

Without a bargain made, the marshal had threatened the sheriff with the power of the Federal law unless he turned young Mr. Grey loose.

This Rinky Dink most seriously considered.

His morality was that of a man who always has taken whatever appealed to his eye. It was also that of a man who, whether from the strength of nerve or strength of will and honor, never had found it necessary to break his plighted word.

In short, he felt that he lay under an obligation to the marshal, and he was one who loved to discharge an obligation generously. If it were a blow, his custom was to return ten for one. If it were the graze of a bullet, a shot through the heart would be about the proper recompense. If it were the loan of a horse, the gift of two good ones would about make things equal.

These were the ways of Rinky Dink, not simple, but exceedingly clear.

When he came back to the jail, the big sheriff stood for a while at the door to his jail.

"You know, Rinky," he said. "You know how it is."

"Sure I do," said Grey.

"You know that a man has gotta have something to say where his say don't belong, even."

"Sure I know that," said Rinky Dink, good-humoredly.

"That's the way with the marshal," said the sheriff. "It don't mean nothing, what he had to say. There ain't no sense to it. Old Mexico, what would it be wanting to say, just because you got arrested on that side of the Rio Grande?"

"Sure," said Rinky Dink. "Old Mexico wouldn't have much to say. She'd be glad."

"That's what I said," replied the sheriff. "She'd be glad. You settle down here. You ain't going to have anything to complain of from me."

30

"No," said Grey. "I think you'll give me the right kind of a hanging."

"With last statements, and pictures, and everything," said the sheriff. "I wouldn't let you miss any tricks."

"I'll bet you wouldn't," said the prisoner.

He smiled at the sheriff, who, nodding solemnly, went back to his office.

There he was taken with a certain illness of ease, in the afternoon of the day. He summoned a jailor and asked him to look to the star prisoner.

"See if he wants anything," he said, dubiously.

The jailor came back.

"He don't want anything," said the jailor.

The sheriff shook his head.

"That's funny," he said. "Mostly, they all want something. They want a chew of Piper Heidsick, or something funny like that. But it ain't nacheral. I mean, for a prisoner not to want something, is it?"

The assistant jailor was amazed to hear himself thus appealed to.

He almost swallowed the plug of cheap Star tobacco which was stowed in the corner of his cheek.

"Sure it ain't nacheral," he said. "I never heard nothing like it."

And he hurried away. Even a close approximation to swallowing a plug of tobacco is slightly nauseating.

The sheriff went home to his dinner. On the way, he found that men had heard, albeit rather vaguely, that he had done something eminently worth while. The moment the sheriff became aware of this, he gathered his blackest scowl and strode along the streets without noticing even his oldest friends.

He knew that a sheriff is expected to appear as a man of dark humor and martial might. He knew that, on this day, he was collecting at least two thousand votes. He felt that he would draw his salary perennially.

He was a good man, and a brave man; but after all, he was only an elected officer.

After dinner he went into his office, a small room which he had made his sanctum.

He told himself that he needed seclusion, and that the harmless pretense of his office gave it to him. In reality, the office was his sandpile, in which he played at various imaginings, such as a second marriage.

This evening, he had just passed through an imagined divorce case and was selecting a wife from an imaginary file of applicants, when a shadow fell across him.

He looked up into the eyes of Lawrence Grey. There was no leveled revolver, no mask, nothing but the youth himself. But the sheriff, although he was a valiant man, did not attempt to snatch out his weapon from the open drawer beside him.

Instead, he stared fixedly at the boy.

"It was that sucker, Jones," he said. "You tell me the truth. It was that hound Jones. You fixed him, didn't you?"

"It was those sucker locks that you use. Birnham and Bixbee locks are the only kind to have in any self-respecting jail," said the boy.

"I went and recommended them in my last report," said the sheriff. "But look at what I've got to put up with in a jay town."

"I didn't come here to talk about the town, or the town cops," replied the boy. "I came to talk about the county, and the sheriff of it."

"All right," said the sheriff. "What have you got to say?"

"I thought that you were on the up and up," said young Lawrence Grey.

"I'm on the up and up, Rinky," said the sheriff.

"You call it that, going body-snatching to the shady side of the Rio Grande?" asked the boy.

"Aw, you know, Rinky," said the sheriff. "That's all in the game."

"It's not in *my* game," said the boy, softly. "I'm on the up and up, too. Only, I'm straight on it. I came here to tell you something. The next time you try a double cross, I come and get you."

The sheriff felt an inward fear, but outwardly he maintained his composure.

"I hear you talk, son," said he.

"You won't hear me talk the next time," said the boy. "What's the price of that five-year-old bay mare that you've got in your corral, back there?"

"Eight hundred dollars," said the sheriff.

"Here's six hundred," said the boy.

He counted it out on the table. He took it from a pocket with his left hand, and he counted it out on the desk. It was all from the left hand. The right had remained divorced from occupation, as the careful sheriff noticed.

For he knew that overconfidence will sometimes make even the wisest relax, and he was watchful to take advantage of such a moment. On the other hand, he was very well aware that Rinky Dink was inwardly praying for some overt move on the sheriff's part.

"Here's six hundred," said the boy, "and that's a hundred more than she is worth. Am I right?"

The sheriff did not dispute the point. He said: "Where did you get it, Rinky? You didn't have a bean, when we got through with you at the jail down-town."

"I rubbed the lamp," said Rinky, mysteriously, and yawned. "That's the way I get everything."

"Yeah, you get a lotta light," said the sheriff. "There's no doubt about that."

He fingered the money with some satisfaction. He had paid two hundred and eighty for the mare the year before. She was worth more now, but hardly this much.

"Which way, Rinky?" he asked.

"Oh, south," said Rinky Dink. "Why?"

"We'll be sorry to lose you," said the sheriff.

"Will you?" asked Lawrence Grey. "Well, that's all I wanted to say. This besides: If you start any gab about a stolen mare, you know, it won't go down."

"Look here, Rinky. Don't you underrate me," said the sheriff.

"I'll try not to," said the boy. "But that was pretty raw—I mean, going over and trying to slam me on the south side of the river. That was the worst that I ever saw."

"I made a mistake," said the sheriff.

"Nothing but," commented Rinky Dink. "Well, just turn your head a minute, will you?"

He had stepped back to the window.

The sheriff turned his head.

"So long," said a voice outside the window.

The sheriff looked. He had expected it, but still he had to rub his eyes.

"So long," said he.

5

Young Mr. Grey went out behind the house and in the barn he took a bridle. He lighted matches until he was sure that it was the oldest bridle in the lot that hung along the wall. Then he stepped into the corral and went, as though he had marked the spot before, to an extreme corner, where he roused a sleeping horse.

It stood up, without a start and without fear. It stretched itself, one hind leg at a time, shrinking its back. Then it poked its soft muzzle into the face of Rinky Dink.

"You come with me, sweetheart," said he, and passed the bit into the mare's mouth as she tried to nibble his fingers.

He jumped on her, unsaddled as she was, and instead of opening the corral gate, he tried her at the bars. She winged her way across them, and landed running, as only a hot-blooded horse will do.

"I knew it," said the rider, softly.

Then he jogged her down to what could only be called the under side of town. He went through several twisting alleys. Once he had to dispose of a yapping dog, a big fellow. This he did by catching the dog by the scruff of the neck and throwing it across the neck of the mare, and over a fence adjoining. The dog landed in a pile of tin cans, made a vast metallic racket among them, and then fled with a whine.

Rinky Dink went on, smiling. He did not court trouble, he always told himself, but when it presented itself, he could not help admiring the virgin's fair face.

He came to a small house with a large back yard, in which two cows were tethered. At the door of the house he rapped, and when the proprietor came out, Rinky Dink murmured a few words that caused the man to disappear and come again, bearing a saddle. This he strapped on the back of the mare, while Rinky Dink stood by and smoked some of the Turkish tobacco, admiring its taste, and admiring the lines of the mare, and admiring himself just a little, also, if the truth must be told.

"You know," said the man, as he finished the saddling, "I'd take this to be the sheriff's bay."

"It is," said Grey. "I bought her from him."

"Bought her from him?" said the other. "Yeah. I'll bet you did. So long, Rinky."

"So long, Boz."

Rinky Dink rode out from town and went down to the river. He stood the mare on the bank and looked down at her image and his own in the water, putting out a star or two.

On that side lay Mexico, like a smoke. On this side, a rider approached him, with the pale sheen of a carbine laid across the pommel of the saddle.

" 'Lo," said the new rider.

" 'Lo," said Grey.

"What's the news?" said the other.

"Tamales," said Rinky Dink.

The rider laughed.

"I mean, what's on your mind?"

"I'm telling you," said Rinky Dink. "Tamales, and frijoles, and tortillas thinner than lace wheelwork, cold as the belly of a fish, and better than Easter Sunday."

"Is that what you're thinking about?" said the other.

"Yes," said Rinky, "and beer, pulque, tequila, mezcal, hot peppers, and cold wine. You know?"

"Yeah. I know," said the other.

He laughed again, softly.

"I guess you're going south," said he.

"Yeah. I'm going south," said Rinky.

"You go around by the bridge, then," said the stranger.

"That water looks like wading, mostly," said Grey.

"Not while I'm looking," said the rider.

"You're a border guard, are you?" said Rinky Dink.

"You can call me that," said the stranger. "You sashay back through the town and hit the bridge, old son. It's all right, only you go over by the bridge. That's all I gotta say."

"The bridge is hard," said Rinky, "and this mare has tender feet."

He reached across. His hand was not much faster than the paw of a cat, when it flicks out at the already captured mouse. He laid it on the barrel of the carbine. With the other hand he laid the muzzle of a revolver on the man's big chest.

"Oh," said the guard, "somehow I didn't seem to recognize you, at first."

"That's too bad," said Rinky. "Which way are you going?"

"*A*-way," said the guard, with the proper emphasis.

"Go right on," said Rinky Dink. "I'll watch you travel. I've got good eyes in the dark."

"What's your name, brother?" said the guard. "I mean, what's your working name?"

"Some people call me Rinky," said Grey. "And some add Dink to it. You can call me either or both. I'm not proud."

"Sweet little piebald Saint Mackerel!" said the guard. "Is that which you are? So long, brother. I never really seen you, taking how dark the night is."

"Of course you didn't," said Rinky. "So long, partner."

And he watched the guard drift slowly down the bank, the mustang that bore him stepping high and light like a horse that still has all its running inside it.

When the man was a dim thing to be guessed at among the distances, Lawrence Grey rode the mare down the bank. When she was belly deep, he let her drink one swallow of the muddy water and felt her shiver.

"She's been raised high," said Rinky Dink, "but she's going to be raised higher."

Then he turned and looked back at the lights of the town streaming over the water. They ran tiptoe, flashing over the ripples of the current. They made the boy think of small flags, streaming and flashing in wind and sun. And the flag he thought of above the rest saddened him a little.

"Some day I'm going to change," said Rinky Dink. "I'm going to get me a brand new name, and settle down, and be a clerk or something—"

He made a sour face in the darkness.

Then he put the mare at the water, and she took it eagerly, bravely.

They climbed the farther bank, the water dripping down from them noisily, and the river moving with a soft whirl and murmur in their rear.

Out of the brush before them a voice said cautiously: "Pedro?"

"No," said Rinky Dink.

And he rode straight up the bank and past the brush, paying no heed. He heard voices murmuring inside the shadows: "That Pedro, he is always late, and he never brings enough. He drinks whisky. We are fools to keep a man who drinks whisky so much."

"A man who did not drink a lot of whisky," said the other, "would never do Pedro's work."

Rinky Dink passed on through the night. He put the mare to a canter and judged her as she hand-galloped and then ran. She was so full of herself that she began to buck as she raced along. Rinky Dink laughed gently, and with the edge of his heel, he ground into her ribs.

She flinched, bending in a half bow, and then she remembered her good manners.

They went on to a small village, which opened out its gathered lights into a wide scattering. He rode through the streets, turning several corners. The warmth of the day was still gathered, fenced from the cool night winds. And the lazy voices of the gossips murmured here and there, and men and women sat on doorsteps with the light from within flashing on moist brown faces. There was a smell partly sweet and partly pungently aromatic and sour, the characteristic odor of a Mexican town.

He felt that he had ridden not miles but centuries south of the border.

At last he came to a house where the door was

unlighted. He halted his horse, and called: "Margharita! Margharita!"

A woman ran out from the nearest house, panting with excitement. "Be still, fool of a man!" she gasped. "There has been a death."

"Margharita! Margharita!" called Rinky Dink, still softly.

He felt rather than saw the woman in her trailing black as she appeared on the threshold.

"Ay?" said she. "Ay, señor?"

He waited a moment, taking the taste of the wooden, wretched voice.

"Margharita, reach out your hand," he said.

He could see the hand, dimly, by the help of the starlight. Into the hand he put a sheaf of bills.

"There are some pesos," said he. "There is enough to keep young Manuelo honest for two years, and by the end of that time, he may stay honest forever."

"Who are you?' said the woman, gripping suddenly at the paper, as though the meaning of it were nothing until she had the touch. "Who are you?"

"You call me several names," said Rinky Dink. "But I'll tell you this. Whatever they say, Francisco was wrong. He tried to sell a man who never had harmed him, and he deserved to die."

"You liar—you sneak, now that he is dead," said Margharita. "Take back the dirty money—"

"Hush, hush," said Rinky Dink. "I am the man who killed him, and who would kill him again. I am not giving you this for his sake but for the sake of the

41

younger boy. Remember me for what I tell you. Remember me and my words, because enemies always tell the truth."

He heard the great intake of her breath.

He reined back the mare into the street, and taking off his hat, he saluted her with it.

"Madre, adios!" said he.

He rode off into the dark of the street. There were children playing in the warm dust, and he had to make the horse weave deftly among them, picking its way with dainty steps.

His thoughts went back to the bereaved mother of Francisco Vittorio and the brutal words he had spoken to her.

He thought of the young Manuelo, also, and his bright face, and the fine width between his eyes. He might be saved to the world, after all!

He rode on until, glancing back, he saw that the lights of the town had gathered once more into an armful, into the breadth of a hand, into a single broken ray.

6

Not in the Mexican newspapers, not in the conversation of the cultured classes, which is rather drenched with French, but in the chatter of the rabble, and in the folk songs, and the tales that live from mouth to mouth rather than from page to page, one hears much of San Vicente.

It is usually referred to in phrases like this:

"White as the walls of San Vicente"

or,

"Shining far away, like San Vicente among its green fields"

or,

"Rich as the golden-hearted water lilies of San Vicente"

or,

"Cool as the cypress shadows of San Vicente."

One gathers, too, so often is it mentioned in the songs and the lays and the tales, that youth in San Vicente is gayer, younger, more beautiful than in other places in this world, that the peon has more leisure, and the farmer more profit and kindness to spend. One feels that music, over its river, sounds sweeter, and that the tremor of strings about the town is never quite still, night or day. One knows that in San Vicente the hour is never too early for ambition, and never too late for love.

The Mexican poet begins charmingly: "When the Creator of All saw San Vicente, he loved its beauty, and he cast his arms about it, and ever since, it has lain within the embrace of the green mountains."

In all of San Vicente there was no more popular gathering place than the Casa Bianca. Up from the river, at this place stood the cypresses in a double row, reaching the tips of their branches in a friendly fashion to one another, and beyond the cypresses there was a ragged and weedy lawn, and beyond the lawn there was an open-armed building of white-washed adobe, like most of the others in the town. In the day, that whitewash looked rather flea-bitten and continually peeled away in patches to show the dull gray of the mud walls beneath. The lawn seemed a trampled, half-dying thing, and under the cypresses, among the tables, there was generally a flutter of paper here and there on the ground, and a disorderly sprinkling of cigarette stubs, more or less smoked. The poor mozos who cleaned up the place swore that the cigarettes grew out of the ground on their own accord, just as rocks grow in the fields of the poorest and most unlucky peons. But at night the Casa Bianca was quite another place.

Then the lawn seemed a glimmering sheet of velvet-soft grass. And the house was dignified and large, and ancient in its look. And by the light of the lanterns scattered among the lower branches of the cypresses, it always seemed that the nobility of the nation had gathered to drink and smoke and gossip, and eat tamales and other dishes so hot that they curled the Nordic tongue.

On this night the scene was a little more brilliant than usual because General Miguel O'Riley was present with most of his suite.

The general, in another land, might have been called Mike O'Riley. But since the family was three or four generations old in Mexico, he had become well nigh as Spanish as all the rest of the land. His skin was as dark. His eyes were as black, and had the same hint of smoke in the whites of them. He possessed a waxed mustache, two double chins, and a large stomach. But in the bursting red of his cheeks and in the sparkle of his eye there was the hint of a more northern race.

He was as gay as the rest, dressed in his uniform which sparkled with the greatest amount of gold braid. But the twinkle in the general's eye seemed to say that he smiled a little at his own magnificence.

General Miguel O'Riley was the chief potentate of San Vicente. He owned the largest stretch of lands. He had the greatest number of peons attached to his estate. He possessed a larger share of San Vicente town real estate than any other.

So he became a general without ever having drilled a company, marched a regiment, or handled a brigade whether in the field or barracks. He was made a general because his adherence was valuable to the regime then in power.

The difference between him and a good many of the other generals was not an important one from many viewpoints. It was simply that he had a sense of humor which three generations of life in a passionate southern land could not quite wash from his brain and his blood.

On this evening Miguel O'Riley sat under the largest of the cypress trees, and around him were grouped four tables. He sat at one, with a friend on either hand. Others sat in larger numbers at the other tables. And all faces, at all times, were turned toward the general.

He had recently returned to the land of his fore-fathers, and since he already spoke English very well, he had come back with something of a brogue, of which he was very proud, and a good deal of the latest slang. The general was one who wished to keep abreast of the times, and his blood being what it was, and his name what it was, the only times that sincerely mattered to him were the times in Ireland. Secretly, he nursed a longing to amass sufficient coin in Mexico to travel to the land of his forefathers, buy a castle and a dozen hunters, and settle down to a life of fox hunting, and the serious drinking of Irish whisky.

All that kept him from instantly selling his fat estate in Mexico was the size of his stomach, which would not sit well on the back of an Irish hunter. Every Monday he determined to reduce. Every Tuesday morning he started the painful process. Every Tuesday afternoon he gave up the task until the following week.

He was always full of good determinations, but he found it hard to translate them to cold facts.

The rest of the general's party was equipped with gold lace in plenty, very much like himself. Most of them held commissions which they had derived through his influence, and they knew as much about military affairs as he did himself, no more and no less, the total being zero. But they were all fond of the general because he was the affluent sun that shone upon them, and he was very fond of them because he knew of their dependence. No Irishman can be unhappy when he is the center of influence.

These people were drinking red wine which was a little acrid but pleasantly cold, and they were eating sandwiches of good white bread, filled with red fire.

The next group worth consideration was a set of five men with gloomy faces who sat one tree beyond the general's cypress. They were drinking tequila out of little green-tinted glasses, which harmonized both with the slight green-white color of the liquid and the raw green fire of its taste. They smoked, one and all, Mexican cigarettes, made like cornucopias, large at one end and pointed to the other. They allowed the cigarette ashes to fall where they might, on their clothes, or wind-blown on the clothes of each other. After a time, the shower of ashes began to turn their shoulders and the lapels of their coats white, but the whiteness was never dusted away.

As they talked, they leaned a good deal toward one another, and spoke very softly. If anyone came too close to their table, he was sure to be received with a silence and two or three black looks, as dangerous as the glinting of bared knives.

These five looked all of a pattern. They all were young—between twenty and twenty-five. They all wore small mustaches, some less successful than others. They all had on broad, gray hats, and they all wore tiny white camellias in their buttonholes. It was easy to see that they belonged to a club. It might be a club of thieves, of night roisterers, or gamblers, of indigent younger sons, of poets, of newswriters, or of revolutionists. The talk might have been of where the next throat could be cut, the next purse taken, the next scandal picked up, the next meter introduced, or the next bomb thrown.

They did not attract much serious attention, but since they so obviously wished to be left alone, the other patrons of the Casa Bianca, on this night, chose tables at least one removed from the table of the five ardent talkers.

The third point where the eye should rest on this occasion was the quietest table of all. It was rather near that of the five youths. And the reason it was so quiet was that it was occupied by only one man.

He was very young, elegant, and handsome. He was well dressed, seemed to have plenty of money— for he ate and drank of the best—and he had been coming to this particular table for seven nights in a row. He was now recognized in the place, and his right to that particular table was established. He did not have to tip the waiters exorbitantly, for in Mexico the rights of habit are recognized almost before any other rights in the world.

No one offered to sit down at his table for the reason that he never spoke a word of Spanish. And he seemed incapable of learning anything. Although the same waiter, on five successive nights, had pointed out the same dishes, named them, sweated over them, gesticulated, brought samples, crowed like a rooster, flapping his arms, quacked like a duck, made the horns of a deer upon his head, and imitated a cow chewing her cud, still the young man from the north seemed unable to understand, and he was always surprised when he saw what he had ordered. He was always surprised, but he was also delighted. The waiters put him down as a fool; but that was to be expected from one with hair so yellow, eyes so blue, and face so pink and white. They put him down also as a good-natured fool, and that made all the difference. He tipped them just well enough to keep them expectant.

This youth might have been a mere traveler, but he was probably attached to one of the mining companies which operated with foreign capital near San Vicente, combing out the ores in the great veins of its mountains. He was probably rich. He was the sort of a patron that one wants to see more of at a place like the Casa Bianca.

No one in all that place, headwaiter, lounging detectives, or scrawny news reporter looking for a story, would have suspected that the table of the general, the table of the five young men, and the pink and white youth from the northland were all to be connected, in another moment, with the worst scandal that ever had occurred in the Casa Bianca. But such was the case.

7

Punctually at eleven o'clock, the circle of five gloomy young men always dispersed. So they did this night, walking off toward the path that led down the river, and most people watched them going with relief. It was only the young Nordic with the yellow hair and the blue eyes who appeared to notice nothing, but with a covert side glance saw one of the five turn back from the rest of the group and return along the margin of the river, where the lights from the lanterns shone with only the faintest light. It was so dim that only the best eyes in the world could have perceived the youth, lost as he was in shadow from time to time, and then half appearing again. But the lad of the yellow hair had eyes as keen as those of a hawk, and he followed that progress.

He put on the table enough money to cover his bill and leave a tip of just the right size, then arose, stretching himself a little, though without raising his arms. And since the night air was turning damp and very cool, he pulled across his shoulders a jaunty cloak, and took a pair of gloves out of the slit side pocket of the cloak.

The orchestra, a little before this, had received from General O'Riley a request for a certain piece, and now, the more to honor him, they approached and struck up the tune near him, all smiling in his direction. The general liked such compliments. They were not particularly delicate, but the general had no great taste for delicacy.

The music was in full swing. It was not of the sort to appeal to a connoisseur, but General O'Riley chose to lean back in his chair a little and half close his eyes, and nod his big head in rhythm with the beat of the piece. This pleased everyone, the musicians, the waiters, and the others who were dining or drinking and gossiping under the cypresses.

This idyllic pause was interrupted by a wild, half-choked cry that shattered the music and brought it to a jangling pause, and one of the men at the general's own table was seen half risen from his chair, his face distorted, one arm stiffly pointed.

Those whose glances flashed in the direction of the gesture saw a tall, dark-clad youth with a somber look and a pair of short mustaches not five yards from the general and poising in his raised hand, with his body bent back a little and tense for throwing, a round, black ball, the size of a small melon.

But it was no melon. They all knew what it was, and men simply cast themselves backwards and rolled from their chairs—all except the general. He also had seen, but he did not stir. There was no time to save himself. And he preferred to meet death leisurely.

This instant in which the cry was heard and the assassin seen lasted the sixteenth part of a second. And then, as the bomb thrower started to fling his missile, a revolver cracked sharply. The would-be murderer twitched half around and clutched at his ruined right shoulder with his other hand, while the bomb, dropping to the ground, rolled slowly on toward the general, as though it had a volition of its own to complete the work which the gloomy youth had commenced.

Now he of the cloak and the gloves and the blue eyes and the yellow hair slid deftly back beneath his clothes the gun which he had drawn, and running forward, while waiters and guests and musicians were scrambling away for their lives, many of them on all fours, he picked up the rolling bomb and tossed it with an underarm throw far out into the river.

As it touched the water, it exploded with a roar that made the flame leap in the throat of every lantern chimney, and set the table services jingling, and sent through the trees a gush of noise like one blast of a powerful gale.

And far above the surface of the river arose a great fountain that stood like a broad-shouldered ghost for an instant, and then melted away into the water once more.

In the meantime, the general and he of the cloak faced one another. Of all within the grounds of the Casa Bianca, only those two had confronted the danger without flinching—the general motionless in his chair, the boy in action.

Now General Miguel O'Riley stood up and made a gesture.

"Seem to be plenty of empty chairs near me," said he. "Won't you sit down?"

The blue-eyed youth bowed.

"I was just going, General O'Riley," said he. "Some other evening I hope to see you again!"

And he walked off with a careless saunter beneath the cypresses, leaving the general behind him with bulging eyes and a discolored face. For O'Riley had so long been the Zeus and the disposer of all graces and favors in San Vicente, that he could not imagine a service performed except for the sake of a reward.

Now he could only gasp to the gendarmes who were coming up on the run.

To one of them he said: "Have that fellow—that American who did the shooting—have him followed—find out about him. And you there—" he roared to the police who were manhandling the wounded bomb thrower, "don't tear that man to bits. He's a fool. That's all. And he's been punished already for part of his folly. Bring him here!"

They brought the youth before the general. They had guns pressed against the small of his spine, and against his sides. He was white with the torment from his shattered shoulder; all his right side was encrimsoned with the flow of blood. The general looked straight into his eyes.

"Who are you?" he asked.

"A man who hates tyrants!" cried the boy, and he stiffened himself, as though he were facing a firing squad that instant.

"Oh, the devil!" said the general, with a groan of boredom. "Another patriot, eh? Take him to the hospital, not to the jail. Give him the best care at my expense, and then turn him loose. He won't throw bombs again."

"Set him free? The murderer!" cried the lieutenant of gendarmes.

"Do as I tell you," said the general. "Every young man is a fool, and this one is the youngest I ever saw. Take him away, and take him quickly. Call Doctor Matazzo. He's the best bonesetter. Take him quickly. The boy is losing blood fast. Gentlemen, it is time to sit down again. Music, strike up once more! The evening is spoiled for only one of the people, I take it!"

And, within two minutes, he had restored the Casa Bianca and its grounds to a perfect tranquility. It was one of the characteristics of General O'Riley that he could be less angered or upset by physical danger than by a badly cooked meal or a poor wine. The music started, the people returned to their tables, and fresh crowds poured in from the streets, first attracted by the roar of the explosion and then by the report of what had caused it. They thronged in, and got tables as close to that of the general as possible.

He enjoyed the scene. The tale of his calmness was repeated on all hands. He was stared at and idolized. And General O'Riley felt that this was one of the few perfect nights of his entire life.

8

It was not that the general's life had been saved, alone; it was that in the same scene he displayed himself as a good deal of a hero. For the first time, in a way, he felt that he could put on his gold-braided and silver-shining uniform-coat with a sense that he deserved to wear it.

He stayed up late that night, sunning himself in the public admiration. When he went home to his big rambling house, one of the few in San Vicente which was made of stone, he found there a little man with pouchy eyes, stained purple all beneath, and clawlike hands, the first fingers of which were deep yellow-brown from the fumes of cigarettes which never left them. The general was glad to see him for this was his own private investigator.

He took him up to his sitting room, which served him as an office for his many affairs.

Without even sitting down, the general thrust his fat hands into his coat pockets and said: "Now, Ortuga, what have you found out?"

"Nothing," said Ortuga.

"That's impossible," said the general. "You're like a bird; your eyes have to see more than those of other ordinary men!"

The general believed in flattery and always used it. He loved it so much that he knew how to apply it to others. Now Ortuga flushed just a little, and almost smiled.

"I only had an innkeeper to look at," said he. "That was all I had tonight. Tomorrow, it may be a different story. I got at everything the innkeeper knew. He was anxious to tell everything twice over, when he learned what his guest had done for your excellency."

"Tut, tut," said the general, relishing the honey-taste of this. "But go on. What did you learn?"

"Only that this seems to be a model young man. He rises at eight every morning. He goes to bed at twelve every night. In the morning he stays in his room, studying Spanish, in which he appears to make no good progress. In the afternoon, he goes to a restaurant and sits for a long time over his meal. In the evening, he walks at the usual hour in the plaza, and then goes to the Casa Bianca. He does these things every day. He is always home not later than eleven-thirty, and he always is in bed by midnight. He seems to have no business except the study of the Spanish tongue. The innkeeper suggests that he is a very good but a very stupid young man. His name is John Lawrence."

"English blood!" said the general, with a scowl. "I hate that English blood. Taciturn, dull-witted, regular. He saves my life and goes home—not to avoid my thanks or embarrassment, but because—it is his bedtime!"

In the morning the general rose early—that is, to say, at ten o'clock—and while he sipped chocolate frothed with hot milk and ate handfuls of sweet bread, cut transparently thin and toasted dry, he received his secretary and listened to the probable business of the day.

The assassin of the night before was now resting easily in the hospital. The doctor declared that his right arm was not necessarily ruined, but that it would be stiff for three years, and that he might feel the changes of weather in it through life.

"Whenever he lifts a glass of wine for three years, he will be forced to think of the clemency of your excellency," said the secretary.

The general smiled. He listened to other details.

A peon had lost his wits and run amok the day before, knifing three of the general's other tenants, but none fatally. The man was now raving in the jail and telling his keepers that debt was a weed that grew two pesos for every one that was paid off! There was an American who had come up from Vera Cruz. He was in haste. He looked like a man worth seeing—but with precautions. Governor Ilvarado was coming to San Vicente in three days' time and sent his special respects. There were five letters begging assistance of one kind or another. Señor Huerta wanted a hundred and ten pesos a hectare for his grazing land, but for cash the secretary thought it could be bought for ninety.

"That American," said the general. "Where is he?"

"Waiting now in hope of seeing you."

"Why do you think he is worth seeing?"

"Because he will not tell any of his business to me."

"How much did he give you in cash?" asked the general.

The secretary looked straight back at him. He knew the general from of old, and exactly how to deal with him in all matters.

"He gave me ten pesos," said he.

The general was not offended. He knew that his servants all accepted bribes. He felt that the bribes were a direct tribute to his importance as a man and as a master. All he objected to was lying and concealment of what his domestics took in. He did not ask them to keep their hands clean. So he smiled at his secretary.

"If he's as liberal as that," said he, "I'll see him here and now. Give me the blue slippers, there, with the featherwork on the toes of 'em. Help me into that dressing gown. So! Now I'll go into the office and see the gringo. You go to Ortuga and learn from him what new things he has found out about the young American, John Lawrence. Then go yourself to the inn at once, and give the young American my compliments and tell him that I trust he will do me the honor of entering my carriage at one o'clock and coming to my house for lunch. Hurry! Until I know something more of that young fellow, I shall not have a moment's quiet in my mind."

So he walked into his office, and by the time he was settled at his official table, taking the rubber bands off a few important-looking sheaves of papers, the American entered. His name was Dickon Jarvis. And the

58

moment he came in, the general recognized the type. For Jarvis was one of those long, lean Southwesterners who speak with a drawl and whose clothes always have a suggestion of dust in the wrinkles.

He shook hands lazily; he smiled on one side of his face; and he was no more impressed by the general than he would have been by a beggar boy on the one hand, or the Archangel Gabriel on the other.

He said: "I've come to talk to you about a man."

"What man?" asked the general. "Sit down and rest yourself."

He was proud of every Americanism he could bring into his easy flow of English.

"He calls himself John Lawrence," said Dickon Jarvis. The general showed not the slightest interest. There was a prickle up his spine, but he knew how to control his face.

"I've heard the name," said he.

"He's poison," said Dickon Jarvis. "I'm here to tell you about him."

"What are you going to tell me? And why are you going to tell it?" asked the general.

"Because the people who sent me down here from the United States are afraid of him."

"What people are they?"

"People that know a thug when they see one," said Jarvis. "This lad is really Don Diablo, if that means anything to you."

"Is he called Mr. Devil somewhere in Spain or Mexico?" asked the general.

"He is. All up and down the river, and a lot of points further south, too."

"What else is he called?" asked the general.

"On our side of the river," said Mr. Jarvis, "we call him Rinky Dink. Some people call him Larry. He has other names. He has more names than coats. He's really Lawrence Grey."

"Then he's wearing one half of the truth down here," said the general. "Before you go any further, I want to tell you that this same Don Diablo, this Rinky Dink, saved my life last night."

"Of course he did," said Jarvis. "And that's why I'm here. He'll use you as a lever now. It's not you he wants. Dead men are nothing in his young life. He's had plenty of them sprinkled along his trail. He broke from jail with a murder charge against him. He's wanted here in Mexico, too."

"Instead of coming to me," said the general, "I should think that you'd call in the gendarmes, if that man is wanted, and you wish to get him out of the way."

"Gendarmes would never get him," said Jarvis calmly. "Gotta have special operators to handle him, or he'll burn his way right through the fingers of twenty men."

"You know where he lives, I suppose?" said the general.

"He lives," said Jarvis, "in a tavern room that looks over a kitchen roof. The roof runs out to a stable that has three loft windows he could get at. Then he could get out of two windows from his room, or he could run down the hall and try the cellar exit, or run through any one of half a dozen other rooms and slide for the street."

"You know all the exits," said the general, "and I suppose that you could get plenty of men?"

"I'd need three good men, at least, at every possible exit," said Jarvis. "And suppose that I march up thirty or forty fellows and start to surround the place—do you think that would work with a fox who never sleeps except with one eye open and one ear cocked?"

The general smiled.

Jarvis briskly continued: "Rinky Dink's a bad one. You never know where he'll be. You never know what he'll do. I've come here and shown you my cards. And this is what I suggest. A man in your position, general, can't afford to get himself messed up with a lad like Larry Grey. After what he happened to do for you last night, he's sure to try to use you. And you're pretty sure to see him again. All that I want to do is mighty simple."

"And what do you want to do?" asked the general.

"Let me slip three men into your house staff. They'll give you security."

"And what will they give you?" asked the general.

"A chance to check him up, wherever he goes and whatever he does."

General O'Riley smiled faintly.

"He saved my life, Jarvis," said he. "Now you want me to sell him."

"I want you to save your reputation from him. That's all," said Jarvis. "And your skin, too, perhaps. I tell you, if Rinky Dink filed notches for every man he's put out of the way, his gun handles would be half notched away. I know the story. He went off last night and wouldn't stay when you asked him to. That's because he knew that you'd send for him today. Haven't you?"

The general shrugged his shoulders. He could not help admitting that it was a point.

"I have to think this over," said he. "I can't make up my mind all in a moment. Will that do you, Jarvis?"

"That'll have to do me," said the other. "But if I could have my way, I'd load a dozen men into your house and catch him when he comes."

"You know, Jarvis," said the general, "that I don't use this house for a trap? However, I'll think things over. Perhaps you're right, but I have to take time. I still can see the lad with the bomb raised. And there's still a roar in my ears—the noise it made when it exploded."

Jarvis seemed to see that he had covered as much ground as possible. He said his adieus briefly, and left the house at once, leaving behind him General O'Riley in a more amiable frame of mind than he had been in for months.

For there was nothing that he loved with a passion equal to his love of trouble. An air thick with plots and counterplots was his ideal atmosphere, and he guessed, now, that this was the air which he might breathe for some time to come.

He thought of the dapper form of John Lawrence, alias Lawrence Grey and several other titles; and he thought of the big, loose-jointed frame of Dickon Jarvis, with his cold, straight eyes. With such men as these entered, a good deal of warmth should be generated before long. And the general loved action when it was hottest.

He was fond of saying: "The bigger the net, the more it catches; and San Vicente is my net!"

Now it was entangling fish which were likely to break the meshes, to be sure, but they would be all the more sport to land.

For one thing, he had not the slightest intention of taking Jarvis' broad hints and betraying the boy. On the other hand, he did not wish to betray Jarvis to the lad. This appeared to be a "gentleman's game" in which a new pack needed to be broken open for every hand. But the general had sat in at just such games before, and he loved them above all others. So he went off whistling, to take his bath.

9

When Jarvis left the O'Rileys' house, he went in his buggy with his span of horses spinning down the street raising a thick cloud of dust behind him as he kept the horses at a brisk pace. As he came to a little shop where morning chocolate and lunches at a cheap rate were served, out under the patchy shadows of a number of umbrella trees, Jarvis pulled up his team, tethered them at the hitching rack, and sat down at one of the little iron tables.

Jarvis had chosen his hour well. For it was before noon, and there was not a soul sitting at the tables in the cool of the trees. He took the table nearest to the kitchen and he gave the kindest smile he could summon to the proprietor. He did not waste time beating about the bush. He said: "Well, Señor Murcio, I came here hoping that I'd see the famous young man who saved the general's life!"

Murcio smiled, a little sadly. And he shook his head.

"He will come here no more," said he. "This will be a good deal too simple for him, now that all the doors in San Vicente will be open to him. He never came, you see, except that he liked to sit under the trees and study his book of Spanish. And then, I could speak English to him. That was why he used to come here."

Dickon Jarvis blinked. He had heard the purest Castilian ripple from the lips of that same young scoundrel Rinky Dink in days of yore.

He muttered, rather choked: "He can't understand Spanish, then?"

"Not a word. Hardly a word," said Murcio. "He has not the gift of tongues. Some men have it and some have not, but God knows that the language makes no difference, so long as the thought is good."

"That's true," said Jarvis. "I can smell those beans. It's a little early to eat, but I have to have a plate of them, and some bread and butter."

These things were brought, and afterwards, Murcio stood at a little distance, smiling in hope, but ever anxious until the verdict was given.

"The best beans," said Jarvis, around a mouthful, "that I ever had between my teeth. The very finest, the best cooked, and the best flavored. You ought to be in Mexico City. You'd be rich, there. But tell me about that brave young countryman of mine. Everyone is talking about him today."

"And why not?" said Murcio, extending his right hand to demand the same question of all-pervading space. "Is it a little thing to draw a gun and shoot a man? And is it a little thing, then, to pick up death like a child's ball, and throw it away?"

"No," said Jarvis, "he must have courage. But they say that he doesn't look the part."

"He looks," smiled Murcio, "like a child that has grown up suddenly. He always seems a little afraid. He used to sit there, at that back table, and his back to the street, too, rumpling his hair, and poring over his book, poor boy, and saying to me: 'Señor Murcio, say again for me—"Hombre"—I never can roll the *r*!' And that was true, for he never could learn it, though he tried for seven days."

"Just sitting there and studying, and talking very little, I suppose?" said Jarvis.

"Not for two or three days," said Murcio. "But then

65

I was lucky, for I struck on a theme that was after his fancy. A theme like a fairy story—the tale of Juan Ray, the great American rich man, the millionaire, who lived such a life here in San Vicente, and ended so strangely."

Jarvis looked suddenly down, lest his eyes should betray him.

"I've heard a good deal about John Ray," said he.

"Who has not?" said Murcio, again asking the question of all the world. "Who has not heard of Señor Ray—except this young American, so brave, so gentle, so charming, and so modest. I felt for him, when he used to sit there with his book, a certain pity, as though he were a little child, and in a terrible world. God knows that it is a cruel world, señor. But now the great general, he will take care of him, of course."

"I suppose," said Jarvis, "that if the boy never had heard of John Ray, he asked a good many questions, eh?"

"Questions? No," said Murcio, "I don't think that he ever asked questions, but he used to shake his head, and exclaim, and his eyes became dreamy as I talked. That was the way with him. He forgot his book. He forgot everything, and sat there, señor, like a child, and listened. When I told how Señor Ray scattered his money, and rescued his friends when they were in trouble, and how the good man never would say no to any who needed help—when I told him those things, he used to sit there almost with tears in his eyes. And then, yes, and then he would ask me the names of the people who at the last turned their backs on poor Señor Ray, after his money was all gone. He used to ask me their names, and shake his young head, and say that they were bad people."

"He asked their names, did he?" murmured Jarvis.

"Yes," said Murcio. "He used to ask their names and frown, as though he were trying to remember them. As if one day he would like to do justice on them."

"One day perhaps he will," said Jarvis.

"What did you say, señor?"

"Nothing," said Jarvis. "But John Ray makes a good subject for talk, well enough. Everybody refused him help, in the end, when he lost his fortune, they say."

"All except Miguel O'Riley," said the restaurant keeper. "He, God bless him, with his great heart, he would not forget such a man as Juan Ray, though he had had very little from that wild, rich man. But they say that he took Juan Ray into his house and showed him the sum that he had in the bank, and asked him what part of it he would use. And Juan Ray would not take a penny, but swore that since the rest of the world had been untrue to him, he would not give the world the satisfaction of paying him money through a single one of his friends. One exception, he said, made the rule. That was just before he died."

"In the river?" asked Jarvis.

"Yes. In the river. His body was found there."

"But I've heard," said Jarvis, "that that body which was picked up never was proven to be his."

"One hears a good many things," said Murcio, "but after all, what was more like Juan Ray than to curse the world, and throw away his life, after his money was all gone."

"That might have been like him," said Jarvis. "But then again, one hears that he may have gone up into the mountains."

"What would he do there?" asked Murcio, gravely. "A man like him, used to twenty servants always about him, what would he do up there among the rocks? No, he would live and die here in San Vicente, I think. When I remember him, it is as he was one day when I saw him riding a stallion at full gallop, bareheaded, under the cypresses, and his long hair was blowing, and his strange divided beard was whipping across his shoulders, and he was laughing as he galloped. When I think of a strong man, though he was not very big, I think of Juan Ray; when I think of a happy man, though he had his sorrow in the end, I think of Juan Ray. And always as he was that day, galloping under the cypresses—"

He paused, shook his head, and went hurrying and hobbling off to the kitchen.

At the same time, a slender young man stepped in from the street under the shadow of the trees. He carried a thin stick that glimmered like a rapier, and he picked his way among the tables until he came to the rearmost table.

68

"Why, hello, Rinky," said Jarvis.

Lawrence Grey turned, and seemed to stumble. At least, he moved suddenly back so that the trunk of a tree was between him and the speaker for an instant. Then he came straight to Jarvis and held out his hand.

"Hello, Dickon," said he. "I'm surprised. This is a long way off your beat."

"I had to move," said Jarvis. "That last deal in Denver caused too much comment. It got breezing through the newspapers. People are getting too excitable, these days—a little safe-cracking and they're all in a buzz. What's brought you down here?"

"Oh, same idea," said Grey.

He sat down at the table.

"I never knew trouble to make you budge before," said Jarvis. "And you've had plenty of it buzzing around. But you've gone and made yourself a hero since you arrived. I've heard about last night."

"The fool stepped right out in the light," said Grey. "He made a picture of himself. Half-witted, I'd say. Or romantic, or something like that. Good beans, aren't they?"

"The best. I've been talking to Murcio about you. Seems you eat here?"

"Every day. By the way, I don't understand a word of Spanish."

"I follow you," said Jarvis, and he nodded to Grey, but also his nod covertly included two men who were drifting by in the street. They turned straight in among the trees.

69

10

Murcio came out with a pot of chocolate for Grey, and waited until the latter had poured out a cup and sipped it, and smiled his appreciation. Then he went back to continue with his anxious cooking, for a thousand successes were never enough to quite reassure him.

Said Rinky Dink: "It's a queer thing, Dickon, that people like to look at themselves while they're eating. Ever notice that?"

A warm content filled Jarvis, for his men were approaching nearer and nearer each moment. Two good men they were. He had brought them a long distance, and he preferred their calm brains and their sure hands to twenty ordinary gunmen.

He began to taste victory in the very beginning; a sudden foreflash of distant results sweetened the mind of Jarvis.

"I've noticed that," said he. "You take restaurants, the way they line the walls with mirrors—"

"Even a little dump like this," said Rinky. "Murcio's pretty clever. He's put a mirror on every tree facing the tables."

"I didn't notice that," said Jarvis.

"They take some noticing, they're so small," said Rinky. "There's one on the tree, there, right behind you, and just in front of me. Every time you move your head, I can see myself behind you."

"Can you?" said Jarvis, bored a little.

"So I can see in the mirror everything that you see," said Rinky Dink.

Jarvis blinked suddenly.

"Can you?" he murmured.

"The other trees, and flashes of the street, looking pretty blinding bright under the sun," went on Rinky.

"I suppose that you can see that," said Jarvis.

"And the two fellows who are sauntering in," said Rinky.

"Yes. There's a couple of them over yonder," said Jarvis.

"If you made a sign to them," said Rinky, "I wonder if they'd fade away to the street again?"

"If *I* made a sign?" said Jarvis. "What d'you mean? What have I to do with 'em?"

"Oh, not much," said Rinky. "Not any more, at least, than I have to do with the gun that's on my knee just now."

Jarvis shook his head.

"You've got a wrong steer, old son," said he. "I'll tell you what: I'm by myself, down here."

"Word of honor?" asked Rinky.

"Yes. Word of honor."

"Look at me and say it again," said Rinky.

Jarvis looked him straight in the eye. It was hard to do, but he managed the trick.

"Good," said Grey. "I always knew that you were a good, first-rate liar, but I didn't know you were as good as this."

"I tell you, that couple doesn't mean anything to me," Jarvis assured him again.

"Well," said Rinky, "you try a sign on them, anyway. Try a sign that'll send 'em back into the street where I can see 'em go. Don't let 'em come a single step nearer!" he added, his voice lowering.

This new note in the voice of Rinky was something between the croon of a child and the purr of a cat, and the eyes of the youth wrinkled a little at the corners as though he were tasting some keen physical pleasure.

Jarvis leaned back in his chair and for a tenth of a second he tried to weigh chances. But his brain refused to work. He made an apparently casual sign, and the two who had come in from the street drifted just as carelessly back toward it.

"That's a good deal better," said Rinky. "And since I don't want to have anything on you, I'll put this away."

Jarvis saw just a glint of steel as the boy's hand disappeared under his coat.

Then admiration warmed the voice of Jarvis.

"You never carry 'em on the hip, Rinky, do you?" he asked. "It's always under the coat?"

"It's harder to get at 'em under the coat," said Rinky, "but they come away more easily. There's some chance of the flap of the coat getting in the way, of course, but not much chance, if you practice. Practice is what it takes, though."

"Yeah. You've had the practice," said Jarvis. "You're slick, Rinky. You're the slickest that I ever saw."

"I'm sorry you had that trouble in Denver," said Rinky.

"Yeah. That was a bust," confessed Jarvis. "I made some cash out of it. But not enough. You never make enough in our game. There's always too many ways to split everything. A few thousand to a night watchman, and a percentage to a cashier, and then your backers, and the boys that do the deal with you. Well, we took in two hundred and twenty-five thousand up there in Denver. And what d'you think I pulled down out of it?"

"How much, Dickon?"

"Forty grand."

"Is that all?"

"Yes. It's pretty thin."

"It's thin," agreed Grey.

"Then out of the forty, I gotta slip five to an old partner of mine that's on the lowdown. And there's another five that I slip to a state senator that's been on the board of pardons for a long while. You know. I never may need to use him, but when the time comes, that's when it pays to have your string hitched onto the bellwether."

"That's right," said the boy. "But you take almost a quarter of a million and you only get thirty thousand clear. That's a pretty big percentage against you."

"Big? It's rotten," said Jarvis.

"And then," said Rinky, "you slip, every now and then, and the house rakes down all bets."

"What do you mean?" asked Jarvis.

"I mean, the zero or the double zero comes along, and then the house cashes in. I mean, the cops grab you and shove you in the pen, for five—fifteen years, or so."

"Oh, yeah," said Jarvis, "I guess that happens now and then."

"Take you," said Rinky Dink. "You're thirty-two. And you're about as smart as they come. But since you were fifteen, between reform school and prison, you've been put away ten years."

Jarvis looked at the other from under lowering brows.

"You know quite a lot," said he.

"I have to know a little bit, here and there," said Rinky. "I was just figuring out the rotten percentage that you work on. You get twelve per cent of what you make, and you only are in the open for forty per cent of your time to enjoy your twelve per cent."

"Look here," demanded Jarvis, darkly. "Are you trying to reform me?"

"I'm not that big a fool," said Rinky Dink, and his smile was a caress.

"I hope you ain't," said Jarvis. "And where do you get *your* easy money, Rink?"

"It's a lot different with me," said Rinky Dink.

"Is it? I don't see where," said Jarvis.

"You don't think, Dick," said the boy. "Look, for one thing, at the way I've kept out of stripes."

"You're young. You'll have your turn," said Jarvis. "Oh, you got the fat head for a while, but when they plant you, it'll be Salt Creek for you, sweetheart!"

Rinky Dink brooded upon him almost tenderly.

"You don't understand, partner," said he. "You're

all wrong and up in the air; they'll never have me in prison long."

"Aw, I know," said Jarvis. "You'll croak yourself, sooner. That old gag!"

"No, I won't croak myself, either. I've never done anything much."

Jarvis gaped at him.

"My God, Rink," he said, "d'you think that I'm weak-minded, or something?"

"Good old Dickon," murmured Lawrence Grey. "I like to see your eyes pop! But that's the truth, Dick. I'm an honest man."

Jarvis suddenly grinned.

"Go on," said he. "I like to hear you. Go on, Rinky. I never heard nothing so good as this before! You're straight, are you?"

"Practically," said Rinky.

"That's why the cops chase you so much, I guess," said Jarvis.

"That's exactly it," said Rinky. "My business wouldn't be worth a damn if I didn't have the police working for me. They give me a run all the time, and that makes the thugs and the yeggs like you, Dickon, think that I'm one of you. But I'm not. I fill my hooks out of the tenderest flesh of you yeggs, Dick. I always have, and I always will, unless I get tired of the game. You're my meat— you and the crooked cashier, and the fake bankrupt, and the smart boy who runs opium and Chinese over the line. I dine on you fellows. You look back. Fellows like you are always the ones I've plucked."

Jarvis looked back. His mental glance unwillingly seemed to be confronted with a series of facts that testified to the truth of the last statement.

"You wouldn't spill the beans to me, if it was true," said he.

"You won't believe," said Rinky Dink. "And if you tell any of the others, they won't believe you. That's the way with them. That's the way with all of you."

Jarvis slowly reddened to the cheekbones. His eyes glowed, also.

"What do you get out of shooting off your face like this, Rinky?" he asked.

"Nothing much," said the youth. "But just for the moment it made me a little sick to be sitting here with you, Dickon. It turned my stomach to think of what a hound you are, and that I'm sitting here, drinking chocolate at the same table with you."

On the face of Jarvis, the flush became blotched with white, the white of rage.

"I'm not good enough for you, Rink?" he asked.

"Not good enough to lick my boots," said the boy. "Tell me who sent you down here?"

"Who sent me down here? Nobody sent me down here. I sent myself down here. And even if I didn't, would I blab to you, because I like your handsome face so much? You got such a fat head, it's a shame, Rinky!"

"You'll tell me though," said Rinky Dink.

"Will you put the money on that?"

"A dollar to a dime," said Rinky Dink, "that you tell me everything you know inside of five minutes."

11

Jarvis leaned back in his chair and smiled with an honest amusement.

"You're wonderful, Rinky," said he. "I mean the face you got—the way you put it over—that's what's wonderful. You've got me all heated up, son. All about nothing. Just talk. What do you think you're kidding me into?"

"I'd as soon kill you as kid you," said Rinky Dink. "And you know I can do it. I'm a tenth of a second faster than you are, Dick. And I'm a little straighter, too. Besides, you're the stuff that I like to go after."

"You telling me why, Rink?" asked Jarvis, his voice suddenly altered.

"Well, I'll tell you," said Rinky. "It's because you're a thug, and such a dirty thug. You look clean, but you're not. I know something about you, Dick. You cheat your friends. I know about the job in Silver City. He was a friend of yours. He'd given you a hand a lot of times. But you bumped him off, and I know how."

"Hold on," said Jarvis. "I know who you mean. You mean Wash Roberts, the fellow that was burned to death, the poor devil. Are you laying that to me?"

"Yes, the fellow who was soaked in coal oil, and a match dropped on him."

"Anybody says I did that lies," said Jarvis.

"Mattis told me," said Rinky Dink. "He told me

77

while he was dying. He told me how Wash Roberts screamed all the while the coal oil was being poured over him, because he knew what was coming. He told me what Wash said, and how he begged, and how you worked slow, so you could hear more of the begging. Yes, Dick, you're exactly the kind I like to go after. I'd like to shoot the eyes out of your crooked head."

"But you don't like hanging, Rinky," said Jarvis, now pale and coldly alert, on the defensive.

"Oh, I wouldn't hang," said Rinky Dink. "Oh, no; because in another moment, I shoot, and they come running out and find you dead, and you've already got a gun in your hand, and when they search you, they find other guns on you. And in your wallet a stack of hard cash, more than an honest man would be carrying around instead of leaving it in a bank. You see how smooth my case will be? You're just another anarchist, like that poor boy the other night who tried his hand at the general. That's what they'll say. The people down here will vote me a vote of thanks. That's all I'll suffer for knocking you off, if you look the job in the face. But you won't let me shoot, Dick. Because you're going to talk. You're going to tell me who sent you down here after me."

A fine sweat beaded the forehead and the upper lip of Jarvis. At last he took his eyes from those of the boy and, drawing a handkerchief from his breast pocket, he scrubbed his face dry.

"You win, Rinky," he said. "I guess you always win."

He said it bitterly, sneering at the table, as though he despised himself for making this admission.

"Go right on, Dick, while you're in the humor," said Rinky.

"You know Pop Swan?" asked Jarvis. He did not wait for the answer. "Pop always had it against you because he said that you knew too much about his business. He said that he lost out in that deal in Santa Fe because you tipped off the elbows. He said that you'd tip off others, and spoil everything for him. His brother is up for ten years already. He blames it all on you, and he put a lot of pressure on me to go after you. I didn't want to, I had nothing against you. But he offered a bale of cash. So here I am."

"You trailed me all the way south, did you?" asked Rinky.

"Yes. It was a hard job. But here I am. It's old Pop you really want, and not me."

"That's a good lie," said Rinky. "But still, it's a lie. Now try the truth."

The other stared at him.

"By God," he muttered, "you beat me, Rinky."

"Begin," said Rinky. "Begin with Pittsburgh—"

"You know!" exclaimed the other.

"Go on," said Rinky Dink. "I want to hear it from you."

He added: "I've spent too much time. Start with Pittsburgh, and wind up with John Ray, or Juan Ray, as they call him down here."

Jarvis fairly collapsed in his chair, slinking low down in it.

"All right," he said. "I guess you know. They sent for me. I went all the way to Pittsburgh and saw that fellow Leach Forbes. You know."

"Well?" said Rinky Dink.

"They'll pay anything. It's kind of in futures, but they'll pay anything to keep John Ray from being turned up. Why, I don't just know. Do you?"

"Yes," said the boy. "But go on."

"They knew that trouble was likely to start from the border. I was sent back to wait in El Paso. I wait there for orders. Pretty soon I have them—to get to San Vicente fast, and when I get there, to pry you apart from General O'Riley, or see that you never get to him. And I'm to put you out of the way, if I can. And if I can't, at least, I'm to trail you, because you may get on the way to John Ray."

"They want you to handle me, and Ray, too. Is that right? If you can find Ray, he goes west, too?"

The other shrugged his shoulders. He was troubled, but he did not blush.

"You know, Rinky," said he. "They offer pretty big money."

"How big?"

"It's fifty thousand to me if I turn the trick. And all expenses, without any questions asked."

"That's a lot," murmured Rinky Dink. "And I think I've had fifty thousand worth of talk out of you already."

"Are you through?" asked the other.

"I suppose I am."

Jarvis stood up.

But he lingered a little, his jaws working, his teeth gritting together.

"You've won this trick of the game, Rinky," said he. "But the game's not over. Mind you, I'm going to take another whirl at you."

"Are you the head of the other side?" asked Rinky.

"Of course I am," said Jarvis.

"They have less brains than I thought, then," said Rinky. "So long, Dickon."

He turned a little in his chair.

"Take care of yourself," he said after the retreating figure of Jarvis.

Jarvis turned a little, and halted an instant.

"What's that?" he demanded.

"I said—take care of yourself," said the boy.

Jarvis shrugged his shoulders.

"I'll do that, all right," said he.

He walked on from the restaurant to the street, and turning down it, he stepped off with a brisk pace.

The sun was very bright and hot. The white dust in the street reflected both the heat and the rays until he was half blinded and half stifled.

He was not at ease, but his brain was working fast and hard. It had been a serious blow, this trick which the boy had taken from him, but he was glad that all the cards in his hand had not been drawn out by the force of Rinky Dink Grey.

There were still a good many items which could have profited Rinky, and none of these were known to the boy.

From the first, it had been clear to Jarvis, as an intelligent man, that in spite of the instructions he had received, the really important point was not the destruction of old John Ray, even if that man still were alive, but the murder of Rinky Dink.

And that murder he was grimly determined to accomplish.

He had felt, at first, a twinge of conscience because he had always admired young Rinky so much, and because that youth flashed across the minds of the lawless in the Southwest as a sort of superior genius and a guiding star. They loved to talk of him, to recount the narratives of his exploits, and to sun themselves in the brilliance of his superior adroitness in all things.

But now the death of Rinky was a passionate determination in the mind and in the heart of Jarvis.

He was turning gradually in his thoughts various plans for the destruction of the boy, and in the meantime, he walked slowly on, taking turns and short cuts to get to his destination.

A voice spoke behind him, calling him by name.

"Señor Jarvis!"

He turned and saw a man with a fat, smiling face, a very rosy brown skin, and slant eyes. He walked with a stick in his right hand, and a little package of brown paper in his left. It might have been a small bundle of sausages; the brown of the paper was a little stained with oil, or grease, in one place.

"Well? Well?" said Jarvis, impatiently.

"You are Señor Jarvis, are you not?" said the brown-faced man, who was always smiling.

"Yes, yes," said Jarvis. "What d'you want with me? I'm in a hurry, my friend!"

"Are you in a hurry?" said the other, lifting his eyebrows.

"Yes. In a big hurry."

"Would you tell me where you are going?" asked the stranger.

"Why I'm—well, what makes you want to know where I'm going?" asked Jarvis.

He looked closer at the other to see whether or not there was the blank look of drunkenness in his eyes.

But he could not make out. It was an opaque but a smiling eye that he encountered.

"Because I had an idea," said the other, "after you had talked to Señor John Lawrence that you might be about to take a long trip."

Jarvis started and frowned.

He looked about him. It was a narrow alley in which he stood, with blank, windowless walls of massive adobe rising loftily on both sides of him. Elbow turns shut off the view from either street. There was no other person to be seen than this rather elderly man with the brown face.

"Not behind you," said the stranger. "Look at me, Jarvis!"

Jarvis looked back at him with a start and an angry exclamation. And as he turned, a thin tongue of fire darted from the end of the brown package which was held in the stranger's left hand and a heavy report struck the ear of Jarvis, a pain shot like a finger of ice through his breast, blackness struck in one solid wave across his eyes, and he dropped face down in the dust, dead.

12

At one o'clock, the general's carriage came to the inn where young Grey was living.

He had returned from the chocolate shop before this, and mounted to his room, and he was found by the moza who summoned him, still busily poring over the Spanish-English grammar, and shaking his head, as though in patient fatigue.

He was not easily made to understand that the general's carriage was waiting for him in the street, but at last, after many gesturings, he nodded, and then washed his hands, and dried them with care. But when they were dry, the fingernails did not seem to him properly groomed, so he returned to give them a fresh scrubbing with a brush.

Then he brushed his hair, brushed the shoulders of his coat, pulled it down at the back, hunched up his coat collar until it fitted a little higher, adjusted his necktie a trifle, took his walking stick, thin and supple as a rapier, a pair of gloves, a soft gray hat, the brim of which furled a little along one side, and with a last critical look downwards at his shoes, he left the room and went softly down the stairs, tapping the edges of the steps lightly with his stick.

The moza and her husband both attended him forth to the carriage. It was driven by a splendid coachman, with a magnificent footman ready at the door of the carriage to hand in the guest, and opposite the footman was the secretary, giving to Rinky his brightest smile and his most graceful bow.

Rinky got in. He put on his hat, settled his stick between his knees, and folding his hands upon the top of it, he directed his gentle, childish smile straight before him as they drove through the streets of San Vicente towards the general's house.

The general's coachman drove with a dangerous speed. That was partly to show off his skill as a driver and partly to show off the quality of his horses, now that he had a passenger worth impressing.

They never turned a corner upon more than one wheel, and yet when they reached the house of the general, the pale secretary was forced to admit that Rinky Dink had not changed color, and had not altered his gentle smile for one instant.

"The nerveless, cold Nordic!" said the secretary to himself.

Then he showed Lawrence Grey into the house, and into the presence of the general himself. The general received him with much courtesy, and as soon as the servants were out of the room, he said:

"We can dine in the garden, or in the house, Mr. Grey."

Rinky Dink observed the general with a smile, but with eyes that wrinkled just a little at the corners.

"Jarvis called on you, I suppose," said he.

The general started. He had used the name "Grey" without forethought. He had not the slightest intention of revealing at once what little he knew of this seemingly innocent and blandly indifferent lad.

Then he remembered. Lawrence was the name under which the American chose to pass.

"I've said too much," said the general.

"No," answered Lawrence Grey. "You've said too little."

O'Riley was miserable. He told himself that he was a fool, and that he had shattered the web, in the first touch, of what might have proved to be the most charming little mystery.

"Jarvis was here," he said, frankly. "But whatever he said is unsaid, exactly as you wish."

The boy smiled at his host again. He relaxed just a trifle in his chair.

"Let's eat in the garden," he said. "In the open air, there's always a little wind blowing, or a rumble from the streets, and one can have real privacy. I need privacy for what I have to say to you."

The general rang, gave the proper directions, and sat down near his guest.

"Whatever brought you to San Vicente," said he, "I am not one to ask you questions. I am simply at your service in every way. Only"—here his Irish eyes flashed—"I'd like pretty well to be into it! However, it's your affair. Use me as you see fit—just so far, and no farther. I ask no questions."

However, it was plain that the effort to keep the questions under cover had raised O'Riley's temperature to the boiling point.

"I can tell you almost everything," said Grey. "I can tell you, for instance, that I sat for seven nights under the cypresses, waiting for the time when I could introduce myself to you."

"Why didn't you come at once?" asked the general. "Why didn't you frankly come and speak to me at once? Why did you wait, my dear young friend?"

"Because," said Grey, "what I had to say was pretty odd. I *needed* the introduction."

"Tell me, then," said the general, "did you think that sitting there for seven evenings would get you closer to an introduction? Are you as patient as that?"

"I had to establish myself as a deaf man," said Grey. "Deaf to Spanish, I mean. After that—it was about the third day—I began to hear things. And especially, I began to hear them from the table where the five young men were always sitting."

"Hai!" cried the general, light breaking visibly upon his mind. "You could speak Spanish all the while?"

"As well as English," said Grey. "So I sat there and overheard a good deal. The table at which I sat was a little distance from the other, but when the wind was down and the music was still, I used to pick up some interesting words, such as 'dynamite,' and 'death,' and 'the general,' and 'idle rich,' and such things. The more I heard, the more I determined to wait. And finally, on the seventh night, I found that it had been worth while."

The general listened, gasped a little, and swore for a full minute in rapid, expressive Mexican curses. There is no language more gifted in this respect.

"You guessed that they were going to try their hands at me, and still you waited? Until that last instant?" he demanded.

"I drew it a little fine," said the boy. "I didn't figure on the rolling of the bomb. I hadn't thought of that. If the bomb had not rolled, I would have had three or four more seconds to get rid of it, and then everything would have been perfectly safe."

The general said nothing. He merely surveyed his guest with an added attention.

"Do you usually calculate your margins down to three or four seconds?" he asked.

"Sometimes one has to," said the boy. "At any rate, everything turned out well, and there won't be anarchists flourishing in San Vicente for some time."

"True," said the general. He hesitated, and then he added: "It seems that Mr. Jarvis must have used small margins, also. But he was unlucky. You know about his bad luck, I suppose?"

And he looked narrowly at the boy.

"Bad luck?" said young Grey. He leaned a little forward. "I know of one bit of bad luck that he had this morning, when he was talking with me," he commented, "at Murcio's little restaurant. Anything else?"

"One more thing," said the general. "After he left you, he was shot through the heart. The murderer has not been found. No trace of him has appeared."

This word of his brought Lawrence Grey suddenly to his feet.

"Jarvis dead?" he muttered. "Jarvis really dead? And this morning!"

He snapped his fingers impatiently, angrily.

"I might have known! I might have guessed it!"

"You might?" asked the general.

"He was too small for his job," said the boy. "Of course they would have had a better brain over him!"

"I don't quite understand," said the general.

"Understand this, then," said Grey sharply, "that if you will help me, now is the time!"

"As far as money or influence or men can help you. Command me!"

"I will, then," said Grey. "My life and another life depend on what I can get out of you. I don't want your money. I don't want your influence. This is what I want."

He hurried the general to the window, and with a gesture he indicated the sweep of mountains that arose outside of the town.

O'Riley waited for the explanation.

"I want," said the boy, "the two hardest things that any man can ask for. I want a guide who knows this country really well. And I want a man to whom I can trust my life. I want a guide who understands those mountains as though he had made them, and with whom I'll be perfectly safe, a fellow to whom you'd trust your own life, your house, your friends, your money."

The general prided himself upon quick decisions.

"I know the very man," said he. "I'll have him here in half an hour. He has been acquainted with me for years. He has mined and prospected in person every inch, of those mountains. He has made and lost such fortunes that money would mean nothing to him, and he is, in addition, the most honest man I have ever seen. I have known him for years, and there has never been a breath of scandal against him. He is a Rock of Gibraltar."

He rang for a servant, and sent the mozo away in haste on the errand.

He would have taken the boy into the garden, but Lawrence Grey said curtly: "I have to sit here in a corner and think. Let me be alone. Every second that runs by me now, general, is spinning me into deeper water and worse danger. You can't help me. Nobody can help me—only that honest guide you speak of, the man who never has done a wrong to anyone."

The general retired to the window without a word, for he recognized necessity when he saw and listened to it. He waited while the long minutes slowly dragged away.

At last, a servant opened the door and announced a name, and the general, turning in haste, exclaimed to Grey: "Here is Mr. Oliver Slade. Here is the man I told you of, my friend!"

Grey rose and faced the door, through which he saw entering a man of middle age, with a good, strong, light step, though he seemed rather heavy of body, with a fat face which was continually smiling. His skin was extremely brown—Mexican brown, in fact—and his eyes were set slanting and seemed opaque, like yellow ivory and green-black jade.

13

The Oriental blankness of Slade's eye and the oddity of the whole cast of his countenance was not exactly prepossessing to Lawrence Grey, but the vigor with which the general had recommended him much out-balanced any predispositions on his part.

He shook hands with Slade, and felt a soft, reluctant hand in his.

Said the general: "I could never recommend a man as I do you, Slade. And, Slade, I never asked you so sincerely for help as I ask you now. Now, tell me in what way I can help you any further?"

"Let me ask Mr. Slade if he can give me a month of his time," said the boy.

"What sort of time do you want?" asked Slade. "But then, you have my time, at any rate, because I'm unable to refuse anything to General O'Riley."

"Good fellow, Slade," said the General. "I knew that I could count on you. Whatever you can do for him is done directly for me, I give you my word!"

"Very well, then," said Slade. "I'll go with you, whenever you say."

"There's one last request," said the boy to O'Riley. "Let me take Slade away, at once!"

In two minutes they were on the street. As they walked, Grey explained.

"The moment we leave this town, perhaps from the very fact that you're walking along the street here with me, you're in danger of your life, Slade. The general says that you know these mountains as if you'd made them; I want to climb every height that overlooks San Vicente. Do you know the ways?"

Slade looked down at the sidewalk and canted his head a little.

"Nobody knows those mountains as if he'd made them," he said. "I'll tell you. I've walked them, prospected them, mapped them, and studied them for years. But still, I don't know them. Old trails break down every winter. New ones are made every summer. There are landslides and cloudbursts and flooding rivers that keep writing new wrinkles into the face of the land up yonder. But I can take you about from place to place, fairly well, I think. Only, I can't say that I know every line in the face of those mountains. No man does—not even the shepherds in their own districts."

The boy nodded.

"By the way you speak," he said, "you show me that you really know 'em very well. You're the guide for me if you'll come. Will you tell me what you want in the way of wages?"

"I've never worked before for daily pay," said Slade, without false pride. "But I'm flat broke, now. I'm glad to pick up money wherever I can. You can set your own price."

"I don't want to underestimate things," said Grey, "and I don't want to make you nervous, either. But suppose we say twenty dollars a day for you?"

"Twenty's too much," said Slade.

"If it suits you, it suits me," said the boy. "We're starting on a trip that may take a month, but I've an idea that it will take less time. What animals do we need?" asked Grey, in conclusion.

"Riding mules," said the other. "They're the best in those mountains."

"Mules are slow movers," answered Grey.

"The surest mount is the fastest one," said Slade. "I tell you, it's mostly straight up and down, and you go zigzagging on trails a foot wide, most of the time. Mules are the thing. They have good ones here that can raise a gallop, too. Spanish mules. From Andalusian stock. The best in the world."

"There's one horse that we take along with us," said Grey. "A bay mare."

"Let the mare stay behind," said Slade. "She'll only be in the way."

"She won't be badly in the way," said the boy.

"She'll have to be led over trails that will take the heart out of her."

"She's used to mountains," answered Grey. "And she won't have to be led, because she'll follow."

"Two mules for riding and two for packing would be the best," insisted Slade.

"Two mules for riding, because the packs we'll carry will be light," said Grey.

"Whatever you want, then," said Slade.

He submitted without sulkiness, but it was plain that he was disappointed.

"You know these mountains," explained the boy, to take the edge from his own stubbornness. "But I know that light luggage makes a safer skin when it comes to a pinch. Less to pack in the morning and less to unpack at night. Can you handle a gun?"

"I can do a man's share of hunting with a rifle," said Slade.

"And a revolver?"

"Revolvers?" said Slade, smiling a little. "I've worn them and I've used them, but I don't take much stock in all the six-shooters."

"Very well," answered the boy. "Let the revolver work go. We may need rifles for something more than deer, though. You understand that, Slade?"

"I understand that you're afraid somebody may bother us," said Slade. "You haven't explained."

"I don't intend to," said Grey. "All you have to know is that every man that comes within sight of us is likely to be an enemy, and an enemy that would, as likely as not, take pleasure in shooting the eyes out of our heads. You keep awake, and I'll keep awake, and watch every rock for a head popping out behind it, and, every bush for someone peeking through at us."

Slade merely nodded.

"You have to do that, anyway, in the San Vicente mountains," he assured Grey. "You know, the mountains up yonder are spliced together with outlaws and thieves of all kinds. It's a hole-in-the-wall country. They've always been up there. Every revolution sends another sprinkling. And every thug in the country, some time or other, hides out from the law yonder. If you have special encmies, well, that means a little more trouble. But you have to keep your eyes open, anyway, hobble your cattle at night, and act as though you were in Indian country when the tribes are on the warpath."

The boy nodded.

"You're going to be just the hand to see me through this business," he told the other. "You get the mules, will you? What price does a man pay, down here?"

"A hundred dollars a head for good riding mules. Two hundred for animals that will go where mountain goats go."

"That sounds high."

"Not for what you get."

"Then get the best. Here's the money, and enough over for two small packs—blankets, saddles, and whatever men need, traveling skeleton light. You know the idea."

"I know," said Slade.

He took the money which the boy extended toward him, counted it, and put it carefully away in a wallet.

"I can have this stuff in an hour," he said.

"Can you make it half an hour?" asked Grey.

"Time means as much as that, does it?"

"Yes. Every minute counts, particularly to get us out of this town."

"Ready, then," said Slade.

"Very well. I'll work fast. Where do we meet?"

"At my tavern."

He gave its name. They parted at once, and Grey went to a store where everything from a stiletto to a fine shotgun could be bought.

He selected two fifteen-shot Winchesters, and a brace of Colt six-shooters, together with an ample stock of ammunition. He returned to his tavern, made up his pack, got the bay mare from the stable, and brought her saddled to the front of the tavern in time to see Slade come up with two mules. They looked like any other mules, at the first glance, with narrow shoulders, and long ears. But a second glance showed that their legs were perfectly straight at the knees and hocks, and they had not the hanging belly of the usual heavy-feeding mule. Their eyes were bright and big, and they had an unusual air of alertness.

"I paid six hundred for the pair," said Slade. "Where one goes, the other will follow. They've been worked together for two years. And they know these mountain trails around here. They'll hear a landslide begin long before our ears will catch the sound of it. They'll stay fat on thistles, and they'll never give up their work."

"You've learned a lot about 'em in a short time," said Grey, smiling.

"I learned it," said the other, "from the Mexican who owned them. He looked as though he cut a throat a day, but he cried when he saw me take that span away from him. Real tears. Those mules will be right!"

"We start now," said the boy, and straightway the packs were made up, and they started off.

Each of them rode a mule. Behind them, without a rope to lead by, wandered the bay mare. She followed them close and faithfully through the streets of the town.

So they left San Vicente, and began the long climb to the mountain heights.

When they had gone to a little distance, Slade looked back toward the town, which was growing together, smaller and smaller, and Slade said: "Well, whatever we're up against, we're between the two troubles now, I suppose?"

But the boy shook his head.

"The trouble may be under our feet, right now," he answered.

14

As the afternoon wore on, they advanced through the rolling foothills. The sun, now that the wind was shut away by the hills on all hands, beat down with great force. They had mounted above the level of the green plains, and here they were in a world of rocks and cactus. Now and then came a scattered grove of pines, but they were mounting to a region waste and desert.

They had talked very little. Grey had told his companion frankly that he did not intend to discuss the object of the expedition. He wanted a guide, simply, and the guide was to know simply that they were likely to be riding constantly under the bright face of danger. That was all.

But now, as the strength of the sun diminished a little, Slade opened the conversation. He did not speak of the goal of their expedition, but merely remarked: "Tell me, Grey. Did you ever get much use out of a revolver?"

"Some," said the boy.

"I've never seen them do much execution. I've been long enough in the West and in Mexico to see all sorts of barroom brawls, and seen plenty of Colts in the air at the same time. But what was smashed was chiefly crockery and windows. The ceiling and the walls were pretty well ripped up, as a rule, but I can't say that I've seen more than chance wounds."

"No?" said young Grey, quietly.

"No," said Slade definitely. "The point is that, as it seems to me, a rifle is slower, but a lot surer."

"Yes, a lot surer," admitted Grey.

"And as for the revolver," said the other, "I've heard a great many tales about some fellows who can knock a hole in a tin can, or break a rock when it's thrown in the air. But I've never seen it done. Have you?"

"Yes," said the boy.

"Have you, really? Who did it, then?"

"I've done it myself," said Grey.

"Come, come," said the other, still smiling in his usual good-natured manner, but obviously doubtful.

He leaned out from his saddle and picked up a few small stones that lay on the top of a boulder which abutted on their trail.

"Let me see it done, will you?" asked Slade.

"You're a doubter, are you?" answered Grey. "Well—throw the stones up."

"There goes one," said Slade.

He tossed it into the air some ten paces in front of them. It was of a good size, and one could see it turning slowly over and over in the air.

"That's too big to make a test," said Grey.

And, as he spoke, he fired almost without giving his target a glance.

The gray stone disappeared into a puff of dust.

"Good!" said Slade. "Very good, indeed. Nothing much for a rifle—but I'd hardly believe it of a revolver. However, of course shooting at a man is not at all like shooting at a helpless rock, even if it's falling through the air."

"You have three more," said Grey, smiling in his turn. "Throw 'em all."

"Will you pick 'em out of the air, all before they hit the ground?" asked Slade.

"Yes."

"Without fail?"

"Yes, without fail."

"Well, then, here you are," said Slade, and rising a little in the saddle, he hurled the stones high, high into the air, and well before them.

Grey did not fire in haste.

He waited until those trembling little targets were at the height of their rise. Then he fired.

One stone disappeared.

He fired again, and missed. The third shot snuffed out the existence of the second stone, and a fourth blew to bits the third rock before it touched the ground.

Then he commenced to reload, paying no heed to his work, the fingers operating quite independently, as it were.

Slade, in the meantime, was nodding his head and frowning seriously.

"I've been a fool," he said. "I've lived too long in Mexico, and begun to doubt everything. I see that the thing's possible, right enough."

He shook his head again.

"I'm almost willing to believe in the ambidextrous fellow who can do these tricks right- and left-handed, according to the storytellers. Can you, Grey?"

"I can't hit stones as small as those," said Grey. "But at the same distance, I could hit stones say—the size of a man's heart, every time, without failing."

He did not speak with pride. It was a simple fact. He had proved it too often. His life had depended upon that skill.

"I won't ask you to demonstrate," said Slade. "I take back everything that I've been thinking on the subject."

They fell silent, and Rinky Dink was wondering if there were some hidden reason that had made his companion so extremely interested in the matter of the revolver play. It might have been a purely innocent doubt and curiosity, but Grey was in a cynical humor.

He decided, then, that he would watch his guide as a hawk watches the mouse in the field far below it.

They were too busy, from this point on, to do much conversing. The trail was now heaving steadily up among the mountains, and the early evening found them, about sunset time, well up on the face of the San Vicente range.

It was Grey's theory that somewhere upon the mountain tops which surrounded the town he would be able to come upon John Ray in a place where he could live simply, like Timon the misanthrope, but in view of the place where he had lived the happiest and the richest years of his life. From such a place, every day, he could curse human kind, and San Vicente's population above all others.

After that view back into the plain, at the town and the river, they went down a narrow, darkening gorge and came out into a fairly pleasant valley, where the ground was obstructed with many rocks but plenty of good grass for grazing, and where cattle and sheep were dotted about on the landscape.

A crossroads village lay before them, the lights beginning to wink like bits of gold through the twilight.

"There's an inn, down there," said the guide. "Do you want to try it?"

"An inn?" said the boy. "Inns are good places to get one's throat cut."

"That inn?" Slade laughed. "Why, they're the most honest, stupid people in the world," said he. "These mountaineers around here are a solid breed. They don't dig for gold with knives. They try to clip it off the backs of their sheep. Money that doesn't come out of wool or mutton they wouldn't consider real. You'd be safe enough there!"

So Grey consented, and they rode straight on down to the town, with the bay mare still following cheerfully behind them. They found the inn as it had been described. It was built as an adobe house, with the same ponderous, massive walls, and clumsy arches. But since stone was the readiest building material at hand, it had been used in the place of mud and grass, and the inn was a great mass of masonry, the blocks fitted together with the nicest precision.

Here they dismounted and stabled their horses.

15

There was a great bustle to receive them. Everyone in the inn turned out for distinguished foreign guests. There was the host, his wife, his eldest son, and three or four younger children. There was the one moza of all work, and the boy who attended to the stable and was, at once, porter, messenger, wood chopper, and general roustabout.

These people first unsaddled the mules, and when the saddles and bridles were off, they crowded about the stalls where the animals were placed and held up a lantern to admire their points. They judged mules with a shrewd and practical eye, and the consensus of their opinion was that one mule was worth two horses, for such a district as they lived in.

Grey was glad to get this unsolicited confirmation of Slade's opinion. And, in fact, when he looked out at the towering, rocky slopes that hemmed in that little valley, he could not help feeling that the feet of a horse were much too big for any real service. Yet he took good care of Doll, the mare. She had carried him on such a long march that she had become more than a horse—she was a friend to him. He rubbed her down with a few wisps of hay, and himself saw that her portion of hay had few weeds and no moldy spots in it. He sifted out for her a good, clean portion of oats, and poured it into her feed box.

The stable boy, gaping at this care bestowed upon a dumb animal, stood by holding the lantern, and Slade also watched.

"She's sort of a mascot, I suppose," he commented. "Like a dog, eh?"

"Well," said Grey, "if ever I need one burst of speed, I can get it out of her. And out of the mule I never could. I may never need her here in the mountains, but I would almost as soon be without a gun as without a horse that has plenty of foot."

They went back into the inn.

The landlord was very proud of his best chamber, to which they were ushered.

"You like it?" said Slade, seeing the smile with which the other enjoyed the room.

"I like it a lot," said Grey. "All that I dislike is the fact that we have a roof over our heads. Stars would be safer—a lot safer, Slade."

The latter shook his head.

"Well," he said, "if trouble comes our way, you have that pair of ambidextrous guns!"

It seemed to Grey that the other was smiling a little, as though he still failed to take the matter of revolvers very seriously, in spite of the shooting exhibition which he had witnessed on that day's trail.

They went down to the little dining room. It was as

good a meal as Grey ever had tasted, though he had had many a counterpart of it in Mexico.

After that, they went up to bed.

The night had turned cold, with a strong mountain wind whining through the chinks of the shuttered windows, and moaning near and far. They went to bed, snuggled down deep under the goatskins, and young Grey was soon asleep.

But he slept lightly, as he always did. There was some truth in the saying that one eye was always open and one ear was always cocked.

It was shortly after midnight when he wakened, with all of his senses instantly alert. There had been a mere whisper in the room.

He waited.

"Grey!" said the faintest of whispers on the farther side of the room.

"Yes," said Grey, in a lowered voice.

"Did you hear it?"

"What?" asked Grey.

"Voices down there—voices from the stables. Whispering voices, by thunder. Why should people be out there murmuring at this time of night?"

Grey bent his ear.

The wind had fallen dead away. There was not a breath, not a touch of a breeze. Utter silence weighted down the old inn, and yet the cold of the night had increased steadily until it was freezing.

"Do you hear?" asked Slade, in a cautiously lowered voice.

"Nothing," said Grey.

"There's something down there, though," said Slade. "I'm wondering if someone may have admired those mules a little too much. I think I'll go down and have a look."

"I don't think they'll steal the mules," said Grey. "Go to sleep, man."

"No," insisted Slade. "I'm going down."

There was a loud rustling of bedclothes being thrown back.

"Nonsense," said Grey, springing from his bed at once. "If anyone's to go, I'll go down."

He could not let a man so much older go out into the bitter chill of that night. But he cursed silently the nervousness, so unexpected in this fellow.

"Don't you do it," said Slade, protesting. "I'd as soon go. My skin is as thick as yours."

"I'm up already," answered Grey. "Where's the light?"

"There on the small table, nearer the foot of your bed than mine."

"True," said Grey.

He found matches in his pockets, and next, he fumbled with a cautious hand until his finger tips touched the icy cold of the lamp chimney. He laid hold on it with his left hand, and with his right he struck the match.

The flame began to spurt and as suddenly died. So, with a mutter of complaint, he picked up another match.

"Cheap things, these Mexican matches," commented Slade, from the other bed.

"Mighty cheap—no good at all," said Grey.

Then, with the second match ready in his fingers, he paused an instant.

In that single spurt of fire from the first match, he had had an odd impression that the door of the room was wide open, leading into the hall. It could not very well be, because he had both locked and bolted that same door when he went to bed. And yet there was that strange feeling that the door had been ajar, just now, like the open mouth of a great beast, silently gaping at him.

A little chill ran up his spine, and it was not all the effect of the icy air of the night.

"I've got some Swedish matches over there," said Grey. "I'll get hold of them in a moment."

"They're the best," agreed Slade.

But when the boy moved, it was not toward the bed and his discarded clothes, but in the direction of the door.

His bare feet felt the way. They found the hushing, warm surface of one of the goat skins. His out-stretched left hand followed the line of the table. Desperately he cast his mind back upon the picture of the room as it had been when he entered. And he remembered that as he stood in the door that the very corner of the table had been before him. From that corner, he judged his way. It should be about three strides. So he made nine small ones, and then, with the revolver which he carried under his left arm night and day grasped in his right hand, he reached out for the threshold of the door.

His bare foot struck cloth, cloth warm, as if with the heat of a human body!

16

A gun spat fire in the very face of Grey. He struck a sweeping blow with the revolver in his hand, but instead of managing to reach the head or the arm of this man in the dark, he felt the stroke taken on a cushioning of soft flesh.

At the same time he threw himself forward and grappled with a writhing form on the floor of the hall. They whirled over and over. The revolver, striking the wall, was knocked from Grey's hand. He had no advantage of strength. This fellow who wrestled in the dark was as powerful as a bull, but the slight weight of Rinky Dink was reinforced by all that the science of wrestling could teach him. In an instant, he had located the other by touch as though a light were cast upon him, and a second later he had clamped on a neck-breaking half nelson.

It was broken! By the only maneuver known to wrestling, it was broken, and with amazement he realized that he had a trained athlete in his hands. Where could the bandits of these mountains have obtained such a schooling in catch-as-catch-can?

He was so bewildered that he made no sudden move to regain his grip, and with a wrench and a fling the under man twisted from him and spun to his feet, running.

At the same time, he heard the hoarse shout of Slade and felt, rather than saw, his roommate rush past him and down the hall.

Leaping to his own feet, he was in time to see, by the dull night gray of a window that opened on the hallway, the form of the fugitive, swaying as the fellow struggled to get under way at full speed, and behind him Slade, his hands empty, rushing as fast as he could run.

He could have cursed Slade's blindness in dashing down the hallway without a weapon, at the same time that he felt a thrill of admiration for the bulldog courage of the man. He could understand, all in a flash, now, why General O'Riley had been so willing, on short acquaintance, to trust everything to the hands of Slade.

As Grey sprinted in pursuit, he saw the pair whip out of sight at the head of the stairs. He saw Slade apparently leaving his feet in a headlong dive. There was the sound of a dull, heavy blow, and then Rinky Dink, taking the same turn, stumbled over a prostrate form that stretched across the stairs.

He saved himself with hands and feet as he turned over in the air. He landed on the platform where the stairs turned, and down he went. For he could hear the fugitive before him.

The house was up, now. He heard voices shouting everywhere, and as he raced down the lower hall after the dim shape before him, a door opened, and the bulky form of his hostess stepped out in her nightgown. Rinky could not help the collision. It cast the poor woman headlong back into her chamber, screeching at the top of her lungs. It sent Rinky staggering back against the wall, and by the time he regained his balance and could start, he heard the heavy door slamming in front of the tavern.

He did not pursue any further. He waited one instant, and then the noise of hoofs went rattling off up the valley. That night murderer was gone.

Lanterns came tossing in the dark of the corridors, like bright ships in a stormy sea. When the gringo guest was recognized, they swarmed about him. They laid their hands upon him, and all asked questions at the same time.

He picked out the host.

"Send these people back to bed," he commanded, "and come up the stairs with me. My friend has had a fall. He may be badly hurt, for all I know. This whole thing is nothing but a little attempt at murder."

The host yelled half a dozen orders, but he was totally unable to command his frightened, babbling family. However, he ran with his lantern up the stairs behind Grey, and together they found Slade.

He was lying head down along the steps with blood running fast from an ugly gash along the side of his skull. When they picked him up, he groaned a little; by the time they had stretched him out on his bed once more, his wits had returned.

"Dived for the rascal on the stairs," said he, "and I missed him. Confound him! Cracked myself up a bit, but I'm all right, except that there are some cathedral bells ringing in my brain. Otherwise, there's nothing wrong with me at all!"

Rinky Dink murmured a vague reply, and looked carefully at the wound.

Perhaps it should be sewed. Perhaps a mere bandage would be enough. He asked the host, hopelessly, if there were any sort of a doctor in the village.

"There is better than a doctor," said the host. "There is Padre José."

And straightway he sent his oldest son scampering to fetch the man.

"A priest," said Slade, sitting up on his bed suddenly, "is not likely to know much of these things."

But the host smiled with a calm conviction.

He said: "Padre José is not a priest. He is not a doctor, either. He is everything. When he comes, you'll understand!"

"He's their local medicine man, I suppose," said Slade to Grey. "Every village community generally has one or two around. They'd rather go to them than to accredited doctors. They're cheaper, for one thing, and they give you a lot more fol-de-rol for your money. However, we'll let this Father José have a look at the cut. Some of the rascals know herbs very well. Things that help along the healing of a wound."

Father Joseph came in the course of an hour. He was very brown, but his complexion was rather that of a white man who has been tanned by exposure than a Mexican born dark. He had an ugly face, smooth shaven, with a thin, eagle's nose, and eyes buried beneath very deep brows. His chiefly distinguishing feature was a bush of white hair that fell as far as his shoulders and was kept out of his face, Indian style, by a band of cloth tied about his head. In his dress, he might have been the poorest shepherd. The gray woolen cloak that hung over his shoulders was turning green with age; every atom of the nap had been worn from it, so that the surface was like canvas.

He spoke to Grey and the hurt man curtly, in extremely good Castilian Spanish; then he looked to the wound. It would close, he said, if the patient remained quietly in one place for a few days. If he continued to travel, the lips of the cut should be sewed together, and he was willing to undertake the task.

Slade looked to Grey and the latter, with a wry face, declared that it was better to wait.

"Time counts with you, man," protested Slade. "I can't let you waste it on me, in this way. Let the old chap sew up the cut. I'll be able to ride as well as the next one."

But Grey was firm. He felt that the events of this night had proved the mettle of Slade down to the ground, and he was unwilling to allow him to take any risks. After all, as he pointed out, the sewing might cause an infection, and they were far from a place where an infection could have the proper care.

They communicated this decision to Padre José, and he nodded.

He had a broad sheepskin belt about his hips, with several pouches attached to it. One of these he opened, and unfolding it, showed several small parcels inside, wrapped up in thin tissues. Of these, he selected one, and dropped part of the contents into a small portion of hot water. A strong, pleasant aroma spread through the room. Then, washing the wound carefully, he pressed the lips of it together, laid over it a compress soaked in the liquid he had prepared, and then skillfully wound two bandages about the hurt, one crossing it longitudinally and the second at right angles to the first, passing under Slade's jaw.

"You can talk," said the healer, "without parting your teeth. And you can eat once a day, when the bandages are changed."

"Who will change them?" asked Grey.

"I," said the shepherd, "if you will come out to my cottage to live for three days. At the end of that time, if he is careful to do what I say, the wound will be sufficiently closed so that one bandage will hold it. And he can wear a hat and begin to travel."

The host plucked Grey by the arm.

"Go with him!" he said. "There is more wisdom in an hour of his talk than in a year's schooling under good teachers."

"Where do you live?" asked Grey.

"A mile from this place," said the shepherd,

"among the hills. It is a beautiful place. You will be quiet there, and at peace."

"Peace is what we want," said Grey to Slade. "And I'd rather be away from this place than in it. They've followed me closely enough to this point. They'll have less of a chance at me if we're in the open air."

Slade said, shaking his head a little, and speaking without difficulty through his teeth: "You'll have to get that idea out of your head. It was simply some mountain bandit, old fellow. Nobody from San Vicente tried that trick."

"No mountain bandit," said the boy, "is likely to know how to break a half nelson. And no mountain thief is liable to understand the workings of a lock as well as that fellow did. Have you looked at the lock? It was either opened from the inside, which it wasn't, or else there was a master hand at work on the outside. He was an exceptional chap. Witness the length of time that he took entering the room. A crude bungler would have been well inside long before that. But the master waited. No, no, Slade. That visitor of ours was an expert in his business. I know enough about it to recognize the signs of the proficient. He came from San Vicente, and soon we're going to have them buzzing like mosquitoes around our heads. You mind what I say!"

Slade seemed only half convinced. He even smiled a little.

Smiling was the habit of this man. It amazed the boy to notice that nothing in life seemed very important to Slade. He had made and lost so many fortunes, that he was in the custom of taking all mortal events very lightly.

So he smiled now at an adventure which had nearly cost him the fracturing of his skull.

But they accepted the shepherd's proffered hospitality, and made their preparations to remove to his place in the morning.

Before they left, another event took place almost as strange as the attempted assassination in the night: the host absolutely refused to take a penny for their food and room. His guests, he said, were as his family. And since they had suffered an attack while in his place, a debt was owing from him to them, instead of vice versa. They could not prevail upon him to accept a penny.

17

When they arrived at Father Joseph's camp in the early morning, they found the roughest scene imaginable. The land on which he grazed his sheep was at the mouth of a gorge that opened upon the main valley. It was the most broken land that one could imagine, being partly covered with great rocks, and partly with a straggling growth of trees, big pines which formed dense groves in places, and again stood in twos and threes. The grass grew where it could in this rough place, and the sheep and a few goats grazed on it, wandering high up the sides of the steep, rocky walls that enclosed the cañon.

This ravine looked north, and since it was comparatively narrow and the walls were high, it received little sunshine during the course of even the longest summer day. Among the shadows, therefore, the shepherd had built his house.

This hovel consisted of one room only. It had not even a window, but only a door—that is to say, an aperture closed with a flap of skin, like the tepee of an Indian.

As they came up to the place with their host, a young fellow jumped up from the doorway, where he had been sitting cross-legged, and came running to meet them, his bare brown legs flashing. He began to wring his hands and wail when he was still at a distance, and when he reached Father Joseph, he was fairly dancing in impatience and misery. He was a handsome lad but now his fine features were distorted with grief.

Lawrence Grey knew Spanish perfectly, and every sort of Mexican argot and slang, but he could make out of the tumultuous uproar of the boy nothing except that a devil, or "the" devil, had come to him the day before and told him that he would eat his heart if he married Maria.

Father Joseph replied merely: "Go find him, if you can, and bring him here. You come with Maria, too."

And the wailer ran off hastily down the gorge.

Padre José looked after him, shaking his head as he saw the flying huaraches of the runner, but he offered no explanation of this scene, and they now went into the barren house.

Said Padre José: "You"—pointing to Slade—"will sleep in here, because the cold night air might be bad for your head. You better lie down now, and be still. Your friend and I will sleep outside on beds of pine boughs."

"I won't turn you out of your house," answered Slade.

Father Joseph smiled at him with singular sweetness.

"The whole valley is my house," said he. "What you see here is but the most miserable room in it—"

And he waved his hand to indicate all that was in the place.

"Take it," said Grey, in English, to his traveling companion. "You may as well. This fellow is a sort of an anchorite or a saint. The more you can take from him, the more reward he thinks that he'll get from heaven. What do you eat here, father?" he asked, for they had started without breakfast.

"I have a great many vegetables," said Padre José. "Then there is goat's milk, and some good cheeses which I make out of their milk, also. I sell the cheeses in the village."

So they arranged to stay for three days—three of the strangest days that ever were spent by human beings. But in the beginning, nothing could have been more peaceful.

The first thing that Grey did was to go off up the valley with his rifle. He had gone a quarter of a mile when, stepping from woods into a little open hollow, he saw half a dozen deer grazing.

They lifted their heads and looked at him as though they had been cows and he, with his rifle at his shoulder, hesitated. He did not know whether to take the towering buck, or the plumper doe, or one of the little ones.

He ended by lowering the rifle, for they had lowered their heads and begun to graze again. Only one of the fawns romped to a distance.

Tame deer? In this wilderness of mountains?

He stretched out his hand and approached. They would not quite let him touch them. The stag shook his head threateningly, when the man came too close, and held his ground like a hero.

So Rinky turned and went thoughtfully back toward the house. He shot two fat mountain grouse as he went, picking off the stupid birds without any trouble. These he brought home to the hut of the shepherd, and asked the man if the deer were really tamed.

Father Joseph shrugged his shoulders.

"No one shoots the animals in this valley, my son," said he. "You see, there is a curse on killing. If I had seen you take your rifle with you when you started walking, I should have warned you. However, since you've killed nothing but a pair of wretched birds who often do damage in my garden, I think it's no great matter. But shall I tell you the story of the curse?"

Grey sat on the doorstep; Slade lay sprawled at ease inside. The lower bandage was not too tight to permit him to hold a pipe between his teeth, and he was smoking comfortably.

Old Father Joseph, in the meantime, was rubbing up soaked corn into a fine meal for the making of tortillas. He had a rough stone slab and the heavy stone mortar for the work, and he went at it very heartily.

"There used to be a very rich family up there, at the head of the gorge," said he. "You go up to the head of it, and then climb rocks that are like a giant's stairway, and when you come to the top of the stairs, you see a broad plateau, all covered with shrubs and rocks. And in the near distance, you see half of a great house. The other half is gone. It has been knocked down.

"You will notice another thing," went on Father Joseph. "That house is backed against a high cliff, which shuts away the heat of the south wind. And this is the story.

"Once there were two brothers, the sons of that house, and they loved the same woman. The elder one married her, but the younger lived on in their house, and hated his brother more every day. At last, they went off hunting, riding their fine horses, and when they came back, only the younger brother was alive, and he carried the body of the older brother strapped across his saddle. He said it had been an accident with a rifle, while hunting.

"They laid out the body, and that night, while the

widow was praying beside the corpse, a storm blew up, and a cataract of rocks and earth shot down from the cliffs and smashed in one half of the house. It broke the roof over the head of the praying wife, and buried her, with her husband.

"That was a judgment of God, they say!"

"A pretty hard judgment," said Grey. "What had the young wife done?"

"Well, who can tell?" said the shepherd. "Perhaps she had not always looked straight ahead. But I know nothing of that. The younger brother, Fernando Garcias, who loved hunting more than he loved life, from that moment gave up guns. And he forbade any shooting in any part of his estate. If he knew that you had killed these two birds, he might do you some harm, except that you are my guests. However, from that time on, no rifle has been fired at the deer. They have learned to know that this is friendly ground."

"I suppose that poachers break in, now and then?" suggested Slade.

"Something bad always happens to them," said the shepherd. "So now the people all say that there is a curse on the head of the man who uses a gun here in the valley, and the lands above it. That is what I wanted to tell you."

"That fellow Garcias," said Grey, "still lives up there?"

"He lives a strange life," said the shepherd. "After the death of his brother and of his sister-in-law, he swore he would never marry. But to give the world a woman as lovely as the dead girl, he went away and found a pretty little child, and came back and adopted it, and now he raises her like a daughter. He has lost his money. Bad weather kills his crops. His tenants steal from him. He lives like a beggar. But he is raising the girl. She is a woman now, and there is no other like her. You see, my friends, how evil may bring forth good from the mind? So Fernando Garcias has turned evil into good."

"Did he murder his brother?" asked Grey.

"Who can tell?" said the shepherd, with a strange indifference. "And now there is a little work for me to do. Do you see them coming?"

He pointed down the valley, where three people were coming toward them.

18

There was a man on a small horse and a girl riding a mule, both following that same fellow who had been there before, appealing to the shepherd.

He explained the matter to Grey.

"That man on the horse," he said, "is a wild youth called Cordoba. He has done a good many bad things, and he knows too much about guns and knives. You can see the flash of his conchoes, even now, and the glimmer of the gold on his sombrero. On the mule is little Maria. And that is Juan Gil, whom you saw here before.

"Juan Gil was to marry Maria, but after everything

was arranged, in came Cordoba and told Juan, the other day, that he would cut his throat quietly if the marriage took place. Now they are coming to me, so that I can arrange it for them. I must be the judge."

Grey chuckled.

"You'll have to give a hard lesson to Cordoba," said he.

"Perhaps," said the shepherd.

"Do they all come up here for your judgment?" asked Grey.

Slade, filled with interest, got up and came with his bandaged head to the door of the hut.

"You see how it is," answered Father Joseph. "Suppose that a man goes to a court of law? Then it is a long journey. There are lawyers to be hired. The poor people sell half their land to pay for the costs, and they break their hearts for two years before they know the decision. But if they come to me, it costs them nothing, and the thing is settled, one way or another, at once. This is a thing that I don't wish to do. How can one man be a judge over another, and do it wisely? Why, it is impossible. But still, it seems to be a burden that is prepared for me, and so I accept it. If I cannot say what is good, at least, I try to say what is not bad."

He spoke so simply, so utterly without pride in his position, that young Grey looked on him with a new eye.

The three now came up, the man dismounted, and Juan Gil took Maria under the elbows and swung her

122

to the ground. She made a curtsy to Padre José, and blushed for the benefit of the two Americans.

"These are two very wise friends of mine," said Padre José. "Speak before them as you would speak if we were all alone. Who is accusing? You, Juan Gil?"

Cordoba was a man like a hawk, thin, narrow-shouldered, with a bright, cruel eye, and a very dark skin. He was a man of some dignity, as well as splendor in his presence, and he wore his flashing clothes as though he had been accustomed to them from birth—as an ancient king would wear robes.

He now turned his eye with an instant's flashing regard, to each of the three faces before him, and finally looked aside at Juan Gil.

The latter was staring at him defiantly.

Cordoba pointed to him.

"He wants to talk," said he. "Not I! Go on, Juan Gil!"

Juan Gil got himself into a passion without more ado. He pointed out that he had fixed upon pretty Maria five years before, when he was fifteen and she was twelve, and that he at that time had told her parents he would, on a day, with the grace of God, marry her, and that they had smiled and shaken their heads. For he was poor as a beggar, and his parents before him.

He, however, had not been discouraged.

For five years he had worked practically day and night. He constantly had added to his flock, and had erected a good house. Then he had gone to the parents of Maria and taken them out to see the work he had performed. They had broken down at once, and sworn that he should have her.

That was six months ago. The matter had been arranged. Everybody knew that he was to marry Maria. And then fell the stroke of black danger and misfortune.

This man, this devil, this scoundrel, this known taker of purses and cutter of throats—deny it if he dared!—this same Cordoba here had come and promised to kill him the night of the marriage. This was the truth and the full truth.

Father Joseph turned to the defendant.

"Now, Cordoba," said he, "is there any truth in all of this?"

"Yes," said the other, calmly. "It is all true."

"You promised to cut the throat of Juan Gil?"

"Yes."

"You want Maria, is that it?" asked the shepherd.

"Yes," said Cordoba. "I want Maria, of course."

His calmness sent a tingle through the spine of Grey.

"Have you got a herd of cattle or a flock of sheep to support her?" asked Father Joseph.

"No," said Cordoba.

"Have you any land, either?" asked José.

The answer was remarkable.

"My hands are not very strong," said Cordoba. "I could not work as a farmer. Besides, I cannot stand wet feet and cold winds, the way a shepherd must stand them. I could not do any of those things."

"Have you money saved?" asked José.

"No, I have no money," said Cordoba.

"Then why do you covet this girl, when you're in no condition to support her?"

"Well, I could support her," said Cordoba.

"Tell me how?"

"With this, for instance," replied the calm bandit.

And he touched with a light, yellow-brown finger tip the haft of a knife at his belt, and again, the handle of a revolver.

Father Joseph turned to the girl.

"This man, Juan Gil, loves you and wants to marry you," he said. "So does Cordoba. What have you to say about it?"

She had stood like a doll, wooden-faced, during the accusation and the pseudo-defense. Now she opened her great eyes at Father José.

"What have I to say?" said she. "My father and mother have already spoken. I am to marry Juan Gil."

"Then why have you done this to Cordoba?" asked Father Joseph.

"I? What have I done to him?" asked the girl.

"Look at him," said José.

She turned her head, but just as her eyes met those of Cordoba, those gleaming, uncanny eyes, that ugly and impassive face, her glance dropped. She grew crimson.

Father Joseph said: "You want a wife, not Maria, Juan Gil. You love your sheep and your house and your land, not Maria. And if you married her, she would run away from you inside a year. Then you would have all the expense of a new marriage. Would that be any good to you?"

Juan Gil gaped, but could not drink in this news.

Said Father José: "Look at her, blushing. She loves Cordoba."

"Father Joseph!" shouted Juan Gil. "Cordoba is a bad man!"

"That's why she loves him, of course," said Father Joseph. "You go home and forget about her."

"I shall die!" cried Juan Gil. "For five years—"

"You'll have one night of bad sleep," said José. "Then you'll remember your sheep and your fine new span of oxen. You'll go to work again."

Juan Gil wrung his hands.

"I have sworn to her father—" he began.

"Oh, Cordoba will take care of all that," said Father Joseph. "Now go away quietly. You have said enough. Everything will be as I said."

It amazed Grey to see the boy take this judgment as though it had fallen from the sky. He turned and went with an uneven, fumbling step and a fallen head.

From Cordoba's hand the fuming cigarette dropped. He was pale, and he trembled.

"Father Joseph," said he, "do you believe in me?"

"I do, my son," said José.

Cordoba looked to the sky, stunned.

"Sacred God!" he whispered.

He did not thank Father Joseph. But he helped

Maria into the saddle on her mule. He took the reins of the horse over his arm, and down he went along the ravine, walking at the side of the mule.

"See," said Father Joseph, "what children we all are!"

19

When Father Joseph had taken his spade and gone out to work in the vegetable garden, his two guests talked together about him.

Said Slade: "Is that old fellow real, or all fake?"

"What do you think?" asked Grey.

"All fake, except that he's shrewd, and knows herbs," said Slade.

"What makes you say that?" asked Grey.

"Because nobody's as wise or as good as that," said Slade. "We're all partly fakers, and he's a faker like the rest of us. Look at him living like a hermit up here. As a matter of fact, when his face was fat, he was a lover of good living. Look at the wrinkles around his eyes. They're not all there from worrying and praying, I tell you. He got some of 'em in the small of the morning."

Young Grey left the house, a little later, and looked behind the house, but his host was not there. He went down toward the creek, sauntering idly.

When he returned to the shack, he was amazed to find that his companion was not there. Slade had vanished.

It seemed impossible that he could have gone off of his own volition. Who, then, could have compelled him?

He set about the task of hunting for signs, and he found them almost at once.

The shoes of Slade were almost like moccasins. That is to say, the sole was of soft leather and sewed on flat, without any allowance made for a heel. He said that in his work, prospecting among the rocks of the mountains, he usually found it much safer to walk and climb in shoes like these.

And, some twenty yards from the door of the hut, in a bit of softer earth, Rinky Dink found the mark of such a shoe, pointing outwards.

He cast straight ahead, and fifty yards off, he found the mark again, pointing up the gorge.

Up the gorge, accordingly, went Lawrence Grey. But after a time he lost the traces. He cast on boldly, cutting from side to side, but the trail petered out under his nose, and he could not locate it again. He kept on, however, though very soon he could guess that he had gone farther than Slade would have walked. He continued until he found the gorge pinching together, with more naked rocks and fewer trees, and so he came to what had been described to him—a sort of giant's staircase down which the creek plunged with a great roaring, dashing its waters into a fine, flying spray. The trees to the lee-ward of the falls were drenched and Rinky went up the windward side.

Even there the rocks were slippery enough, and encrusted here and there with green mold and mosses. It was a stiffish climb, but at the top he had a reward, for he found a broad, flat plateau, with only a hint of a valley through which the upper waters of the creek flowed. Far away he saw the front of Garcias' house, and he could make out the wrecked half of it, from which the gigantic rubble of stone had been only partly cleared away. He could trace the slide, which had fallen upon the lost wing. The thing looked as though it had happened but a moment before, as though the dust were barely settled, and the rest of the casa might be wrecked the following second.

There was a well-marked trail leading up beside the creek, which wound directly toward the house, and this trail he followed.

In spite of his alertness, he nearly blundered into and spoiled a pleasant picture, a moment later, for as he rounded a great boulder, near the edge of the water, he saw in a little clearing beyond, a girl sitting on the ground, with a swarm of fully twenty squirrels about her.

One sat upon either shoulder, others were in her lap, and a big fellow stood up on her knee and ate something which he held between his paws.

Lawrence Grey felt that he had come to the end of the world; he remained transfixed and staring.

20

She was dressed almost like any peon's daughter. She wore the plainest of dresses, unstockinged legs, and she wriggled her toes in the straps of the cheapest sort of huaraches. There was only one discordant note: a heavy golden chain was thrice looped around her neck, like a narrow collar.

She was feeding the squirrels. He watched her slim hands moving among them, very slowly. The downward cast of her eyes and her solemn, unsmiling lips gave her a melancholy and thoughtful air.

He hardly knew that she had looked up at him, when he heard her saying: "It's all right. You can walk along. They won't budge away for you."

He canted his ear to the voice, it was so low and husky, rather as though she were recovering from a cold. He had a strong physical sense of pleasure from the sound of her speech.

Then it occurred to him as strange that she should speak English. He took off his hat to her in greeting.

"You've been in the States," he said. "You talk like it."

"No," she said. "I haven't been in the States. But I had a rare good stroke of luck, a few years ago. A good handy gunman was run out of Texas, and got down to San Vicente, and he heated up San Vicente, too, until it was about boiling, and so they gave him a run that landed him at our house. He stayed on for a long time. He almost lost a leg from an infection that set in. In fact, if it hadn't been for Father Joseph, he *would* have lost his leg. As it was, he had to stay long enough with us to polish up my English a bit. But as soon as he could hobble, he borrowed a mule from us and drove north again."

"Stole a mule, you mean?" suggested Grey.

"We thought so, at first. But after a while, he sent us down three times the price of the mule. And after that, whenever my birthday came around, and Christmas, and Easter, he used to send down big sums of money. He said he was doing very well at his trade. We never knew an address to write to him, though, and tell him that we couldn't take his money. It's all laid away and waiting for him."

"What's his trade?" asked Grey.

"Bank robbing, mostly," she replied, calmly. "And sometimes he does a little counterfeiting. But he says that counterfeiting is a bore, because it takes so much time, and one has to have such a plant. Perhaps you know how it is?"

"No. Not exactly," smiled Grey. "What's the name of this fellow?"

"He called himself Leonard Smith when he was here," said she. "I don't know his name. He was red-headed, and he had a good, hearty laugh. He was wild to get back to his own country again."

"To hunt for money again?" asked Grey.

"No, not that. But he was a king, d'you see, like this squirrel here. And it happened that another fellow up there had elbowed him out of place and knocked his crown all to one side, and blacked his eye a little, so to speak. And he wanted to get back at him. He used to practice snapshooting for an hour a day with his revolver. It was a wonderful sight to see him."

"Who had bumped his crown askew?" asked Grey.

"A fellow he called Rinky Dink."

She laughed a little, looking before her at the image of the redheaded man.

"Rinky Dink's a funny name, isn't it?" said she.

"It is," said Rinky.

"Well, my redhead hated Rinky Dink."

"Because of the black eye?" asked Rinky.

"No. Because this fellow Rinky Dink is a frigate bird. A pirate among the pirates. He robs the robbers. And Leonard Smith thought that that was pretty low."

"I suppose that it is," said Rinky, "in a way. It's against the rules of the profession. This chap you speak of, it seems to me that I may have met him. He had a small mole under his right eye, didn't he?"

"That's the one! What was his name? Leonard Smith?"

"Yes. That was Leonard Smith. Also, he was Missouri Slim, and Goodtime Harry, and Harry the Hop, and a lot of other names."

"He was good fun to talk to," said the girl. "And how he hated Rinky Dink. When he said good-by to me, he asked me to pray that he'd beat Rinky. I've done it ever since. I've prayed every night."

"Hard luck," said Rinky.

"Why?"

"Well, I was just thinking of the wasted time."

"Wasted?"

"He met Rinky a few months ago," said Rinky. "And he had a lot of bad luck."

"Horrible!" said the girl. "What happened?"

"It wasn't Missouri's fault," said Rinky. "He did his best. He had a couple of friends along with him, and he came in behind Rinky when Rinky was sitting in at a game of poker. But it happened that the chap opposite to Rinky was a good friend and he kicked Rinky under the table, so Rinky did a rolling-side dive for the floor and started shooting."

"What happened?" asked the girl.

"Oh, it was pretty much of a mess, all around. But it was hard on Missouri. He's only wearing one arm, now, and that's his left. Poor Missouri!"

"He came in behind, did he?" asked the girl.

"Yes," said Rinky. "Missouri was always a very careful sort of a fellow."

21

She lifted the squirrels rapidly to the ground.

"Are you going on to the house?" she asked.

He stood beside her. She was quite tall, and he regretted that he had not a few more inches. As it was, there was no question of looking comfortably down upon her. Her eyes, it seemed to the boy, were upon a level with his own, and he carefully kept himself to his full height.

"I'm not invited," said Grey. "I just came up the valley from Father Joseph's place. I thought I could have a look at things."

"Come on," said she. "Father's always glad to have a stranger or two around. He likes to sit down with pipes and beer and talk about things. He likes to gather news. He only gets outside about once in three years."

Grey was glad to go along, and since the trail was reasonably wide, they could walk abreast most of the time.

He said: "Is this a good life? Do you like it up here?"

"Oh, you know," she answered. "It's all right. There are some mules and horses to ride. We have enough to eat and plenty of firewood to keep us warm after the snows begin. It's all right for me while I'm still in school."

"You go to school, do you?" he asked.

"I mean," she said, "it's all right while I'm getting ready to break out."

"What do you mean by that?" he queried.

"What every young person means," she answered. "You've had your break. You've exploded. That's why there's a contented look in your eye, of course. I'll wager that you've done enough to write a book about."

He turned upon her the most innocent eyes in the world.

"I don't know why you should say that," said he.

She snapped her fingers.

"Nobody could know about Smith as well as you do," said she, "unless he'd seen a good deal of the world. Just from talking to you, I'll wager that I could tell you your nickname."

"I don't think you could," he said. "I've never been in this part of the world before."

She laughed again.

"Do you think," she demanded, "that he would have talked so much about you without describing Rinky Dink's appearance, right down to the pink and white of his skin?"

So Grey nodded.

"All right," said he. "I should have thought of that."

"He really came up behind you?" she added.

"Yes."

"Then he deserved what he got," said she. "I'm sorry for him. He made a break in our life, up here."

"And when you explode, as you put it," said he, "what will you do?"

"See things. See people and places, and take the luck that comes my way," she answered. She changed the subject. "Tell me about yourself. What do you do in the world, Rinky? Did Smith tell me some of the truth?"

"Well, what did he tell you?"

"Oh, he told me that you are what he called 'slick.' He said that you could fade out through a six-foot stone wall, or float in through a keyhole. He said that you could turn a glass of water into a six-shooter aimed at a man's heart. He said a lot of complimentary things about you, Rinky. Or should I call you Mr. Dink?"

"Rinky's enough for me," he said. "I'll tell you what I do. I just ramble around and take things easy. But I travel light. Is that the house, ahead there through the trees?"

"That's the house. I'll hunt up Father for you," said she, as they came into the patio. "You wait over in that room. I may have to spend ten minutes or so locating him. There are some books and things over there. Sit down and make yourself at home."

She left him there and he, taking note of the patio, decided that he never had been in a place more down at the heel.

He went on through the open door of the room that had been pointed out to him. Inside, the room was fitted up as a library, but there were not many books. He pulled a *Don Quixote* from a shelf. Dust fell out from between the pages as he opened the volume, and half the print was gone. The binding was discolored and warped.

He put the book back. The room appeared a gloomy place to him—a prison, in a way. It had the strong reminder of better days about it—and the hopelessness that exists behind bars.

And this was the atmosphere in which the girl lived!

In his thoughts vaguely mingled all the strange forms and names and figures which had entered his quest—the marshal in the far-off city, the dying Forbes in Pittsburgh, the rascally rest of the family striving to thwart his efforts to find a worthy heir, the mysteriously disappeared John Ray, the distant sheriff, dead Jarvis, General O'Riley, Slade, Father Joseph, even Murcio and the innkeeper, and this Isabella Garcias, this adopted daughter of a dying house.

"One moment of your attention, señor!" said a polite voice in Spanish behind him.

He turned his head, and through the barred window on the farther side of the room, he saw the lean face of Cordoba, squinting one eye down the barrels of a large-caliber shotgun.

22

When it came to taking chances, there was hardly a thing in the world that Rinky Dink would not venture. But there is always the exception which proves the rule, and in his case the exception was shotguns.

He disliked them with a profound passion. They were not his weapons, for one thing. He did not go out to shoot birds, or to try at deer with buckshot. Birds or beast, he preferred a rifle for long-range work, and a revolver at close hand.

Now he simply lifted his arms slowly above his head.

"All right, Cordoba," he said. "You have me, it seems clear."

At the same instant he was thinking of possible maneuvers—of hurling himself backwards in his chair, for instance, pulling his revolver as he fell, and shooting toward the window before he struck the floor.

"No tricks, Señor Grey," said a voice from the opposite direction.

He turned back. Another double-barreled shotgun was leveled toward him from the half-open door to the patio. Blinding white sun slanted into that court, so that the figure of the marksman was darkened almost to a solid black.

He saw a man of middle age, solidly built, with black hair worn very long.

"I am your host, Garcias," said the newcomer. "I came hurrying so that I could pay my compliments at once. I have been waiting for you, señor. I was very glad when my daughter told me that you were here."

"What a little world it is!" said Rinky, admiringly.

"A small world," said Garcias, coming slowly into the room. "But still, large enough for a good many twists and turns. Keep a good aim, Cordoba. There, that's better, now that I'm out of line with your gun."

He had worked his way down the wall, so his gun now commanded Grey from a safer angle.

"Now, Mr. Grey, just keep your arms raised. Turn toward the window, and walk until your breast is against the barrels of the gun. No sudden jumps. No

138

leaps, no throwings upon the floor. We watched you like a trained bird, and expect you to do surprising things. The guns are loaded with double charges, heavy buckshot. They both scatter widely, even at short range. You could not dodge out of the field of one of them, to say nothing of two. A blind man could kill you, my friend, by merely pointing the gun in the direction of your voice, and pulling one of the triggers. There you are. Rise very slowly. That's well! Now walk slowly, slowly toward the window.

"Very good, indeed! Ha, Cordoba! It was a very wise man who told us to use shotguns with him!"

Cordoba's lean, sour face relaxed in a faint grin of satisfaction.

And Grey walked straight up until the double barrels of the shotgun were pressing against his breast.

"That will do nicely," said Garcias. "Keep the hands steadily up, as though you were reaching for something with both arms. I intend to search you. Be very still. I shorten my gun, take it under one arm, and with the muzzles still touching you, and my forefinger around both of the triggers—hair triggers they are—I go through your pockets. And all the while you stand very still. You listen, as it were."

He laughed a little softly, the breath coming out with a whistling sound on the neck of Grey.

In the meantime, with deliberate hands the Mexican went through the clothes of Rinky Dink.

He produced a considerable collection, though Rinky was traveling light. For Gracias found a revolver under either armpit, another inside the band of the trousers, together with a heavy bowie knife, and a small, narrow-bladed dirk, like a stiletto, so keen that its own weight was almost enough to drive its needle point through a victim's heart.

"That's about all," said Garcias.

"I have irons for his hands," suggested Cordoba, outside the window.

"Irons for his hands?" said Garcias. "Irons for these delicate and subtle hands? Tut, tut, my lad! They think nothing of handcuffs. They slide out through them without difficulty. Even through ones made to order. All fits are too big for his subtlety, I tell you. But an end of rope would do well. Pass it through the bars. No, I have some cord with me, which will be better than rope. Watch him carefully, Cordoba. Mind you, this means something to your pocketbook!"

"I watch him," said Cordoba, "as a starving fox watches a stupid mountain grouse. But why did they warn us so much about him?"

"Because they were wise," said the other. "Because they leave nothing to chance. God bless fore-thoughted men like them! Now down with your hands, amigo. Down with them, slowly and steadily, bending the arms in behind your back. That's the very way. You are amiable and intelligent, amigo! I feel sorry for you. This will do very well. Now, Cordoba, I'm about to put my shotgun aside, and tie these famous hands on the middle of our friend's back. While I am working, if he so much as coughs, or twists to the side, or speaks, give him both barrels. Living or dead, he's as much in our pockets!"

"Do you need to caution me?" said Cordoba. "I would send him flying down to hell with joy. By the grace of God, I shall be married on this money. The most beautiful girl in the world is waiting for me, Señor Garcias. Do you think that I could be careless, now?"

"Very good," said Garcias.

He laid his shotgun aside. Then Grey could hear the faint squeak of the rope as one end of it was tied, probably into a slip noose.

He had been forbidden speech, but he risked it, though without stirring in his position before the muzzles of the shotgun.

"Why do you save me?" said he. "If I'm worth as much dead as alive, why do you save me?"

"Because I don't want the girl to hear the shot," said Garcias, frankly. "Women have nerves. Even Isabella has a nerve or two in her otherwise perfect constitution. They have scruples, too. And even she has one or more in her otherwise resolute nature. No, no, my dear lad, I haven't wanted to stain the floor of my house with you. Besides, my employer and rewarder wishes, if possible, that you may be kept alive until he comes to speak to you for a moment. He wants to talk with you, and then he wants to see you die!"

"Very well," said young Lawrence Grey.

Señor Garcias, behind his back, cursed the knot he had tied and apparently started to make a new one.

"And here's poor Cordoba?" said Grey, to the lean-faced man before him.

"*Poor* Cordoba?" said the Mexican grinning. "Well, if I pity myself today, may I never be lucky again."

"Well, well," said Grey. "Let it go. Though I can't help wondering how Father José will make it right with you."

"Make what right?" asked Cordoba.

"You don't guess, as yet?" said Grey, with pity in his voice.

"Guess?" said Cordoba. "What should I guess about a man as clear as snow water?"

Rinky Dink sighed.

"Well," he said, "there's the advantage of having a man with a reputation. And well the two of them knew it when they took you to Father Joseph."

"What two?" asked the bandit, harshly.

"What two?" smiled Grey. "Why, the two who gulled you, of course. Who else?"

"What two?" said Cordoba again, half lifting his glance from his gun to the face of the man he questioned.

Grey's heart leaped violently. But he maintained the calmness of his smile.

"The girl and Juan Gil, of course," said Grey, carelessly. "What did they want except a day to throw you off your guard. It is too late for you to interfere, now. They are safely at the church, by this time."

"Sacred Mother!" gasped Cordoba, blanching.

Then he freshened his grasp upon the gun.

"You think you can take my eye from your breast, señor," said he, "but in that hope you are a fool!"

"Poor Cordoba," said the boy, "do you think that a man about to die would trouble with a wretched devil like you? I pity you, however. You were gulled so easily!"

Cordoba began to pant.

"It is all a lie," said he. "Maria loves me. She had been in a hellfire of torment for fear she would be married off to that empty-wit!"

Grey smiled again.

"Come, now, Cordoba," said he. "In ways that don't touch women, you're a sensible fellow. Do you think that any girl would see much in a scarecrow like you, dressed up in false feathers? Great heavens, man, haven't you a mirror to look in, or a pool to bend over?"

The slipnoose was now fitted over his right wrist, and drawn tight, while Garcias grunted softly with satisfaction. So hard did he draw the cord, that it bit painfully through Grey's flesh.

Cordoba, gray-green with emotion, tried twice to speak before he could manage the words.

"The dog of a Juan Gil," said he, "he knows that I would cut out his heart."

"Poor Cordoba!" said Grey. "Don't you know that two gendarmes are waiting for you now? Two straight-shooting fellows who will take perfectly good care that you don't come near to the newly married pair."

"You lie!" moaned Cordoba.

"Come! What is this talk? Attention, Cordoba!" said Garcias, angrily.

"He's wincing from the truth like a dog from the whip," said Grey. "He's up here hunting for his mistress, while she is listening to the churchbells ringing. Tush, Cordoba, do you think Juan Gil would have taken the thing so calmly if it had not been a put up job?"

Cordoba, his face convulsed, ventured one upward glance toward Grey, as though to seek for some sort of silent confirmation there.

And Grey, that instant, whipped his left hand from behind his body and reached for the muzzle of the shotgun.

23

Who can say what makes the hand fast and the hand slow? It is some mental stoppage, some dam of thinking that prevents the free flow from the subconscious mind to the muscles.

So the Mexican, looking up to the face of Rinky, though set and fixed for shooting at the first suggestion of movement, though he saw in the eyes of the boy a glint of the coming danger, did not pull the trigger over which his right forefinger was hooked.

The least part of a second later he pulled it, to be

144

sure, but by that time the thrust of Grey's hand had knocked the big double muzzles upwards, and both chambers exploded, sending a roar of fumes and shot just over the shoulder of his coat, scorching the fabric and shearing some of it away.

The kick of the weapon, at the same time, almost knocked the gun out of the grasp of Cordoba and jerked him halfway around.

Rinky, his left hand high above his head from the upstroke he had made, whirled on his heel as Garcias with a wild screech of terror and surprise, grappled at him with two strong arms.

So the boy twisted a little in the grasp and brought down the hard knuckles of his fist behind the ear of the man. As a slung shot falls, so fell the hand of Rinky, and Garcias stumbled backwards, his knees loosened and his body sagging, his hands thrust down to prevent his final fall.

Cordoba, outside the window, realized the little trick which had unnerved him, and cursing bitterly, threw away the shotgun and snatched at a revolver. But when his grip was on its handle, he saw his enemy sweeping a pair of revolvers from the tables.

This was enough for Cordoba. He was a very brave fellow, but he preferred a reasonable share of good luck to what was no better than an even chance against such a foeman. His brain had worked too sluggishly, the instant before. He remembered, now, in a dazzling instant, some of the grave words that had been spoken in his hearing about this same lad, and how it was better to take chances with a high explosive than with him.

So Cordoba leaped to the side. He toppled head over heels, but he fell well beyond the angle of young Grey's possible fire. Tumbling to his feet, he staggered into full speed and made for his tethered mustang, behind the house of Garcias.

Garcias himself could not regain his balance. He staggered against the wall and on the impact fell limply to his knees.

This Rinky saw, and instead of making a hostile move against the man, he stepped to the embrasure of the big window, reached through the bars, and taking the shotgun by the muzzles, drew it inside the room.

So doing, in a way he secured himself from attack in that direction.

Even now he did not at once approach the dazed Garcias. Instead, though he kept a steady eye upon the other, as a cat watches a mouse, he slipped to the table, picked up the rest of his weapons, and all in an instant they had disappeared beneath his coat.

He saw Garcias blunder to his feet again, but still he did not redraw a gun. He waited, and Garcias could understand the significance of the pause. It was simply an invitation to defend himself, to do more than defend himself, by making the first move to attack. But he who has been within the claws of a panther, does not relish a new duel with the beast. Garcias merely stared, and waited in his turn, as a man waits for lightning to drop out of the sky.

Footfalls raced across the patio, now, and Isabella Garcias came rushing into the room.

She glanced at the two men, wild-eyed, and then she cried out: "When I heard the gun—I had a wild thought, all at once—but nobody's hurt?"

Her glance flashed from one to the other, and Rinky, watching her and her foster father, felt a queer pinch of the heart, for the older man stood with a gray face to receive sentence.

Perhaps some thought of his own past came over Rinky, then, and some dark memories of crimes in the other days, and sins in this.

But he said: "I've been playing the fool. We no sooner meet than we begin to talk about hunting—because your father came in with this gun—and I start telling him how I got seven ducks with one lucky shot, one time—and there, you see?"

He pointed to the ceiling and shook his head.

"I'm sorry," he said to Garcias, "that such a thing had to happen."

Garcias gathered himself rapidly together. But he felt the coolness of his own face, and the damp on his forehead, for he wiped it off.

"It was a shock, Isabella," he said. "For an instant, with the roar of the gun in my ears—I felt as though something had struck me—"

He laid his hand over his heart and laughed, shakily. Isabella, looking keenly, critically at him, pronounced: "You need a bracer. I'll run and get you a glass of cognac. You look like a ghost—you look ten years older!"

She ran from the room.

And it left Garcias alone with the other.

He even made a gesture with one hand after the girl, as though to stop her; but he changed his mind in time.

He stood before the boy with misery in his face.

"Well, man?" he asked.

"I don't know," said Rinky, slowly. "You did the thing as though you liked doing it. That's what sticks in my throat. You went after me as though I were a wild beast."

He added: "This is your house, Garcias. I came here as a guest of your daughter, you might say!"

Garcias blinked. He grew sicker of color than before.

"Let me tell you the whole truth. You came here not as a man at all. You came here as fifty thousand dollars!"

"Fifty thousand?" whistled the boy. "Fifty thousand dollars to you if you polished me off?"

"Fifty thousand. And two thousand to Cordoba—there's the whole shame. I think I'd do it again—for fifty thousand dollars."

"Why?" asked Rinky. "I thought you'd lived here quietly out of choice? I thought that you'd left the world?"

"I had," said Garcias. "I'd stay here forever. But what of her? You don't know her. Every bit of her soul yearns for the outside world. I would have cut your throat, man, and had no compunction. I would have felt as though the blood that poured out of you were dollars for Isabella."

He looked hopelessly across the room at young Grey.

Then, taking hold of the back of a chair, he lowered himself into it, a half-lifeless bulk. He put his face between his hands. He was shaking like a man struck with a violent chill.

He gestured toward the door.

"This rotten story—she'll see through it. She sees through everything. She knows that there's something wrong. That's why she went out. Not to get the cognac, but because she wants to give us a chance to patch up something. She saw that I was done for. She wants to let us patch up our lie a little. Our hunting lie!"

He laughed again, and his laughter was a groan that racked him.

Then Rinky dipped into his mind, sifted, as it were, a dozen things which he could easily have spoken, some terse expression of disgust, some reference, perhaps, to another day in the life of this man when there had been a "hunting accident."

Instead, he said: "You know, Garcias, that all of us have certain days that we want to forget. Days when we're drunk, let's say, in one way or another. When we're dizzy, and out of our heads. We don't want our friends to remember 'em. We rub them out of our own memories. Well, I've had days like that, and this is one for you. Suppose you forget it. Pull yourself together. Say you had a shock. You felt it in your heart. That's all right. I'll keep a cool face. Do the same for yourself."

Garcias made a gesture of gratitude and misery. And then the girl came back into the room.

Rinky watched her narrowly, but there seemed no hint of anything in her expression other than solicitude for her foster father.

She poured out a glass of cognac for him and then insisted that he should lie down. He obeyed her willingly, obviously only anxious to get away from observation. She took him away, her arm hooked in his, walking with a gay step, and laughing a little at his "nerves." She called to Grey that she would be back in a moment, and she was as good as her word.

"Father's had a real shock," she said. "He's still trembling a good deal, and he's white around the mouth."

"Things that take one by surprise," said Rinky, "they're pretty upsetting."

Suddenly she was looking straight into his face, with narrowed eyes.

"How many thousands of times d'you think that father has had guns go off practically in his ear?" she asked.

Grey shrugged his shoulders.

"Besides," said she, "that shotgun was loaded with buckshot. And who would load with heavy shot around here, where nothing is ever aimed at except birds, and mighty few of those!"

She made a little gesture.

"I saw where the shot ripped through the ceiling," she said. "They would have blown the life out of half a dozen men, as easily as not!"

Here she paused, still facing Rinky.

"Tell me!" she commanded. "What actually happened in that library?"

"A gun went off," he said.

She laughed impatiently.

"I know that things were patched up before I came in. But—*you* were not holding that gun."

"How do you know that?" he asked her.

"You've handled too many guns," she said. "You wouldn't make such mistakes."

"Very well," said Rinky. "That's all I have to say. A gun went off in the library. And no harm was done."

He paused with her at the old patio entrance.

"You might as well talk it out now," said she. "It will have to come out sooner or later, you know."

"I'm going home to ask Father Joseph," said he. "I've been pretty far away, and I'm going to ask his advice."

24

When he was a little distance off, he turned and saw her still at the patio gate, looking thoughtfully after him. He waved his hat to her and went on into the woods.

He felt as he had never felt before, that he wanted help, and he did exactly what he had told the girl he was going to do. He asked Father Joseph for advice.

When he got back to the stone hut—it seemed more of a tomb than a dwelling place—he found Slade stretched on the willow bed, and the boy demanded rather severely why he had left the place. Slade merely grinned at him, and he said indistinctly, through his teeth: "Because I'm a fool, son. The thought of that creek haunted me. I went up the creek and tried that fishing line. It seemed to me that I'd die if I didn't get a hook into that water."

"Up the creek?" said Grey.

"Up a little branch of it," said Slade. "I found a spot where fish had to be. I could see the loom of 'em. But the devils wouldn't come near my bait!"

Grey turned away rather thoughtfully, thinking how much a mere fishing trip had launched. At the door, his back half turned, he made his report: "They're going to make things hum for us, here, Slade," said he.

And he told of his adventure in the Casa Garcias. He left out most of the girl's part. As for the squirrels, he said nothing at all about them.

When he had finished Slade answered: "I see how it is. We've got to start on. If they're as close as that, they'll smoke you out of here in no time. This scratch of mine is nothing. I can walk as well as the next man."

"Slade," said the boy, "you got that hurt trying to tackle with your empty hands a fellow who had been trying to murder me. Do you think that I can let you go now, and turn that wound into a festering sore, with God knows what results? No, no. We'll stay here and I'll keep them off for two more days."

He left the hut to prevent argument, and in the garden behind, he found Padre José patiently working away at the soil.

"I want to have your advice," Rinky said.

"There's nothing so cheap with an old man as words," answered Padre José. "Here's a tree for shade, and a pair of rocks for chairs, and some good turf for a carpet, and a blue ceiling for our chamber of audience. Now, then, my son, tell me what foolish thing you have done."

"I didn't say that I'd done a foolish thing," answered Rinky. "I said I wanted advice."

"No one wants advice," said the other, "unless he has done something he regrets."

"I came to Mexico to find a man. To get him I had to get a guide first. The guide is badly hurt fighting for me. And while the guide is getting well and I stand by, the enemy tries to take my scalp."

"Leave your friend here in the hut with me," said Padre José, "and go on with your work."

153

"I need him as a guide."

"Take another."

"I could get another, but not a man I could trust. Señor Slade has already risked his life for me, like a hero."

"Señor Slade," said the old shepherd, "has the air of a brave man. But still, you could find another guide to help you. It is better to do that than to let Slade be the bait that draws you into a trap, and holds you there."

"I cannot leave him at once," said the boy.

"You could, I think," said Padre José. "There is something else that keeps you here."

"What?" asked the boy.

"What keeps young men?" asked Padre José of himself. "Money, adventure, or pretty women. There is no money here. Of adventure you already have too much. Therefore it is a girl. Did you look a little too closely at Maria? No, she would not fill *your* eye. It is, therefore, Isabella Garcias."

He said it so calmly and quietly that the boy hardly realized what had been said. Then he quivered from head to foot.

"There *is* a devil in you," he said. "You could not have guessed that, Padre José."

"It was an easy guess," said the shepherd. "I saw you walking up the valley. I know that that trail leads to the Casa Garcias. You come home again walking in a trance. What else could it be than Isabella Garcias?"

"I went with her to her father's house," said the boy. "What do you think of him?"

"I rarely think of him," said José. "He is one of God's creatures, I suppose, but somehow I rarely think of him."

Rinky smiled.

"He had a trap laid ready for me. Cordoba— Maria's friend—helped him spring it. They had me cornered, too, as badly as I've ever been, but by a stroke of luck. I managed to get away. A gun went off in the course of things. No one was hurt, but Cordoba ran away. And then the girl came hurrying in to see what had happened, and—"

He paused.

"You said there had been an accident?" suggested the old man.

Rinky exclaimed with utter amazement.

"There *is* a devil in you!" he said.

The shepherd shook his head.

"I have been young, also," said he. "Also, I have been in love."

Rinky sighed.

"Now tell me what I am to do," said he.

"Good advice would never be followed. Safe and sane advice would be for you to leave Slade with me, and hurry out of this valley, and, if you must have Slade, have him meet you at another place when he is healed. But why should one give safe and sane advice to a fire-eater? The fire-eater must have the fire, or die of a spiritual starvation. Therefore I say:

stay here. Meet the dangers. Love them. Accept them. Dance with them when they come. Make furious love to Isabella Garcias. Dream of her. Adore her. And afterwards, let things happen as fate rules they must happen. That is my advice to you."

Rinky looked at him with great eyes.

"You speak," he said, "as if you were already living inside my mind. You speak out of my own heart, señor!"

The shepherd waved his hand. It was brown and callused, but the fingers were nevertheless shapely and slender.

"There is a sort of universality in old age," said he. "Tell me now, my son, what man it is that you hunt?"

"A dead man, it may be," said the boy. "A man named Juan Ray, who was once very rich, and lived in San Vicente."

"Juan Ray?" said the shepherd. "Well, I have heard of him, too, though it takes a great noise to be heard from San Vicente to this place. But that was many years ago. For fifteen years, I have seldom heard men speak of Juan Ray!"

"He's dead, I suppose," said the boy.

"Dead, perhaps," said the shepherd. "For that matter, I sometimes think that we all die not once, but many times. Who is today what he was ten years before? But this Juan Ray is surely dead. When he lived, there was a great deal of talk about him, even up here in the distant mountains."

"He may be dead," said Rinky, "but if he's dead,

why should people offer fifty thousand dollars for my death?"

"Fifty thousand? Fifty thousand dollars?" cried the shepherd. "That is a great sum! Why should they offer so much?"

"For fear that I may find this same man, do you see? They're afraid that I may be able to find John Ray. And, if I did, a great deal of money would come to him."

The shepherd shook his head.

"I try to understand these things," said he. "But, after all, it is a little difficult. If you find Juan Ray, a great deal of money comes to him, and some other people are trying to keep you from reaching him for that reason—it seems a strange story, my friend. Is it a great sum of money, then?"

"Six millions," said the boy, half dreamily. "That's all. Six million dollars. You can turn it into pesos, if you want to. Six million dollars for Mr. John Ray, if I can find him."

The shepherd made a soft, singing sound.

"That would be as much as he threw away, perhaps? Yes, and much more! Poor John Ray! If he could know, he would turn in his grave, would he not? He would turn, and try to rise, and his ghost would come hunting for you and the money."

He added: "And with a great deal of money, also, they hired you to undertake this dangerous trail, my son?"

"Oh," said the boy, "you know how it is with a

fellow. You've said it before. I had to have something to do. And then a friend of mine asked me to do this—"

He sighed and smiled at the same time, thinking of the battered and weary face of the marshal in that far northern city. But after all, the marshal could be called a friend.

He added: "I get expenses, and a little plus. I don't know how much."

"And the game of it?" smiled the shepherd.

"Yes, the game of it," said the boy.

"And now a hurt friend on your hands, and enemies around you, and a lovely girl to go mad about in addition, and treachery, and danger breathing out of the ground—what advice can I give to you, my son? Only this, to rejoice in every priceless moment of your life, for now you are living, and all the rest of the men in the world are dead!"

25

The hoeing was abandoned for that day, and the old shepherd took Rinky through the woods to a berry patch where the fruit was half a blooming red and half a ripe, bursting purple-black. They picked a quantity, until the mosquitoes began to gather in clouds and drove them back.

When they returned to the hut, they were surprised to see the leather flap that closed the entrance torn down and lying on the ground outside.

The interior was dark as the mouth of an inkhorn. It was old José who, with a faint exclamation, ran inside. He was already striking a light when Lawrence Grey entered, and found the place empty.

For Slade was gone, and there were signs of the struggle he must have made when he was swept off. The mattress was gone from the bed and the willow slats themselves were torn and broken, as though he had put his grip on them in the hope of saving himself. Finally, on the jamb of the door they saw a large smear of blood, as though his hand, first wounded on the slats, had fallen here again in an effort to tear himself away from danger.

But Slade was gone!

Rinky, staring about him, felt his wrath rising. And shame got hold of him, also.

He said: "Father José, if I had been here, this would not have happened. I go off with you and pick berries, like a fool, and my friend is taken while I'm away! What sort of a friend am I? What sort of a man?"

"A young man," said Padre José. "That is all. We should only blame ourselves for faults which are not so closely a part of our natures."

Rinky dropped down on a stool and stared at the floor.

"They can't be trailed in this light," said he. "One thing staggers me. Why should they have taken him away? If they wanted to remove Slade, a bullet through the head would have turned the trick for them just as well as the trouble of taking him off."

"Perhaps," said José, "they wanted to extract from him what he knows about you. And they wanted the proper place and the means for torture. They could not tell when you would come back. And they would not want to have you interrupting them, my son."

This suggestion threw Grey into a spasm of anxious misery.

He said: "If they've touched him—if they've harmed him—God help me if I don't have their blood for it! Where could they have taken him?"

"The world is a large place," said Padre José. "It would be hard to find him, I dare say."

"Garcias helped them before," said the boy. "Perhaps Garcias has helped them again. They may very well have taken him up there."

"I don't think so," answered Padre José. "You know that shame, after all, is a strong passion even in a bad man. You have shamed him. His foster daughter before this has suspected some of the truth concerning what happened in her father's house. I don't think that Garcias would plot against you again, or even lend his house to the criminals. And yet, it is very hard to tell. Fifty thousand dollars for your head! Why that is enough to buy a thousand deaths among poor mountaineers!"

He shook his head, and added, "That rascal, Cordoba, I doubt if even he would be still in the work against you. He's a sensible fellow. He might risk one murder to make his little fortune. But I don't think that he would risk two. He'll take the bad luck that God brought him today. Still in his house and that of Garcias is our best place for looking."

"*Our* place?" echoed the boy. "Do you think, Father Joseph, that I'll let you ride with me tonight?"

The old man smiled at him.

"Do you think, my son," said he, "that I have lived such a short time that I still have many hopes before me in longer years? And, besides, is not Señor Slade my guest? Was he not stolen from my house?"

To him, the matter was as clear and as simple as could be. It admitted of no argument, and the boy, after one look at the iron calmness of that old face, said no more.

He simply went out and saddled the two mules.

26

The two riders came slowly toward the Casa Garcias, for they had taken not the easier valley trail, but a far more obscure one that hugged the face of the opposite cliff.

"He loves the girl," said the old man. "There, you see, is the balcony which he built for her at a time when every peso he spent was like a portion of his own blood. A man like that is not all bad. I remember when he planned the thing. He used to come here with me and talk about the building, and how it could be done most cheaply."

It was a good-sized balcony, corbeled out from the

wall on thick stone beams. There was a slanting roof above it, held up by four slender pillars. Between the pillars, there was a network of stone tracery, a delicate and graceful pattern such as one finds in the church windows of the late Gothic style.

Young Rinky looked critically at the wall which arose, without embrasure, sheer up beneath Isabella's balcony.

Padre José said: "What do you propose doing, now?"

"I'm going to search this house in my own way," said Rinky. "An hour from now, I'll try to meet you in the wood nearest to the patio. Is that agreeable?"

"Certainly," said the other.

"And what will you do?"

"I don't know. I may not enter the house, or else I may call upon Fernando Garcias. Good-by for a short time, I hope. If it is good-by forever, God bless you, and make you die in a brave and worthy way."

Young Rinky watched the other riding up the slope, and he could not help a slight sinking of the heart. For never before had he heard death referred to in such a casual and cheerful manner. He had known desperadoes without fear, but they could not speak in this manner of the final end of things. He was half of a mind to follow the old man.

He took the mule back into a nest of high shrubs, then he went again to the wall of the house, beneath the balcony. From a distance, it looked a solid slab, but close at hand, as he had expected from the age of the masonry, he could see a thousand slightly shadowed crevices where the mortar had been chipped away by the innumerable small chisels of time. Here and there stones projected a little, and again there were holes where a portion of a stone had fallen out.

Even so, it was a tremendous task that he had before him. He contemplated it for some minutes, but at last he had mapped in his mind what seemed a possible way to the top. Then he took off his shoes and his coat, and threw them back into the brush near the mule. Finally he began to climb.

It was not nearly so difficult as he had imagined. The most solid portion of the wall was that at the base where, perhaps, it had been a little less exposed to wind and weather. As he mounted, he found more convenient crevices in which to take finger and toe holds.

Still, it was a hard climb. The weight and bulk of two revolvers hindered him, and he wished heartily that he had taken only one.

Halfway to the balcony, he found a deep indentation. The whole outer half of a big stone had fallen away, and there was room for both his feet. There he rested. When his arms no longer ached, he resumed the climb, and presently the balcony was just above his head.

To swarm over the projecting edge of it would have been no difficulty for a cat, and it was no hindrance to Rinky. He climbed up the corner and taking a grip on the pillar nearest to him, with his feet on the balcony's edge, he breathed again.

Now he was at his post, what was he to do, and what was he to say? He must speak with the girl, if she were in her room. But it was not very late, and she might not yet have gone to bed.

So he hesitated for a moment, and then began to whistle the tune of a serenade which was at that time popular in Mexico.

When he had finished whistling the song, he waited for a long moment. He could hear a sigh within the room beyond the balcony, but he knew that it was only the wind.

So he began to sing the song, and sang it through to the end.

But, when he had ended, he heard no response. There was only the continued, secret whisper of the wind.

He tried his hand at a few imitations of birds. He felt that they came very successfully from his lips, and when he had ended them, he waited again.

She was not yet in her room, it appeared. He could have sworn at the thought that he must descend again. But now a voice spoke immediately before him: "Do you think, Rinky, that larks would be whistling at midnight?"

27

He almost lost his grasp on the pillar, his start was so great.

"Hello, there, señorita," said he, unromantically.

"Hello there, señor," said she.

"Here I've gone and risked my neck," said Rinky, "to climb a ladder with no rungs in it, and all I get at the top is a lot of criticism of my whistling. Why shouldn't I do a lark?"

"You left out half the notes," said she. "And the ones you put in were mostly out of key. Besides, as I said before, would a lark be singing at this time of night, loudly enough to wake the whole house?"

"You're critical," said Rinky, "and that's a bad fault. When did you come out on the balcony?"

"I've been here all the time," said she.

"All the time since I came up?"

"Yes. I've been sitting out here all the time behind the vines."

"And let me wait all that time?" said he.

"You might have waited longer," said she. "But I couldn't quite stand the lark business. That's why I spoke."

She added: "I thought you were a robber, when you came swarming up the side of the balcony."

"Hello!" said Rinky. "And you didn't say a word?"

"I have a gun with me," she said. "I'm not an expert with it, but I could hit a mark that's in touching distance. What brought you here, Rinky?"

"You did," said he. "I couldn't keep away."

"You know what I think?" said she. "You're up here on business. What's the business, Rinky?"

"No business at all," said he.

"Come, now," she answered. "You've seen me today for the first time and the only thing that you know is that I have a good sense of humor, Rinky. You can't depend on much else."

"You've laughed at me enough already," he told her. "And now it's time for you to be deadly serious."

"Why?" she asked.

"Because I'm begging for help," said he.

Suddenly he saw her for the first time, the pale glimmer of her face close to the stone tracery. A bar of shadow crossed her, and made her face grotesque, at first. Afterwards, he could half see and half imagine her beauty again.

"I *will* be serious, then," she told him gravely. "What is it?"

"I want you to give me the plan of this house," he answered.

"You'll have to tell me why," replied the girl.

"Because I want to search it, room by room," he said. She was silent for a long moment.

"And I give you my word," said he, "that I would not touch anything in the house. I want to look through it. That's all. I could jimmy a window. I could go prowling. But my time may be short. A man may be dying now, Isabella."

166

"Dying!" she cried.

"A man who already has come within an inch of death for me," said he. "I've had friends before, but never one like that. A fellow I've known for hardly two days. But he was ready to die fighting for my sake."

Presently there came a slight grating noise, and a section of the balcony tracery opened wide.

She stood before it, saying: "You may come in here. On this floor there are seven bedrooms. They all are large rooms. This is the smallest of them all. There is a hall running past them and overlooking the patio. The rooms themselves look out on the gorge, here, and then front close to the cliff the landslide fell from. Is that clear?"

"That's all clear. Seven large rooms, and no small ones?"

"No."

"Where are the stairs?"

"At the farther end of the hall, after you leave my door. They lead down with a big sweep, and they go up with a narrow twist, a little further on."

"What do they go up to?"

"The top floor. That's where the servants live. There are only two now, and some of the rooms are falling to ruin. The roof has broken in in several places. There are only four or five of those servants' rooms habitable."

"And two of them occupied?"

"Yes."

"Very good. Go on. What's on the ground floor?"

"The ground floor is very like this one in arrangement, except that the hall is the size of the two largest of the bedrooms."

"What's in the hall?"

"Nothing except the tatters of some old tapestries and whatnots. They're generally flapping in the draught. The ground-floor rooms are all wider than these, because they don't open on a hall but directly out onto the patio. It's a clumsy arrangement."

"Do the rooms connect?"

"Two of them. The dining room and the pantry. That's all. Otherwise, you have to go in from the patio."

"Is there a cellar?"

"Yes. The house is as deep underground as it's tall above the ground."

"Why is that?"

"Well, there's a small cellar just underground. That's where the wood and the food and such things are stored. Under that, there's another level of cellar, much, much bigger. It's larger than the floor space of the house. My great-grandfather was a collector of wines. He used to ship them up from San Vicente on mule back. All his life he worked laying down a cellar. And he kept digging and digging and making the cellars greater. He dug three times as much as he needed to. It was a hobby with him. He finished the cellar of the second floor, and then he dug out a third floor, underneath. That's how the house happens to have three—"

She, stopped in midsentence. Then Rinky heard the soft opening of a door.

28

With the opening of the door, no light came into the room. Presently a low voice said: "Isabella?"

"Yes, father," she answered.

A heavy step entered the room. Grey saw the pale gleam of her hand as she raised it in a signal for silence and caution. Then she left the balcony.

"Who are you talking to—here in the dark?" asked Fernando Garcias.

"Who was I talking to?" repeated the girl.

"Tell me at once! I heard you speaking English, from the door. Light the lamp, and have no more talk!" said Garcias.

That moment, as he heard the scratch of the match, Rinky parted the leaves at the corner of the balcony, and stepped back among them as far as he could. He drew a revolver from beneath his coat and held it at arm's length, behind his leg.

He was in the worst quandary he ever had known. If Garcias found him, there would surely be gun play. If he killed Garcias in the girl's room, what would be her reputation thereafter?

Sick with trouble, Rinky waited. He saw the broad, dull beam of the lamp sway slowly across the balcony, as Garcias moved from side to side of the bedroom, apparently searching. His foster daughter made cold suggestions.

"You haven't looked under the bed," she said.

"There's the wardrobe, too. A dozen men could be hiding in there. And what of the balcony, father?"

"You won't shake me," said he. "The bees have a way of finding the flowers. I'll trust you, Isabella, just as far as any woman deserves to be trusted—which is, not at all! I love you; I admire you; I am charmed by you; but I trust you not an inch. Now for the balcony," said he, and straightway the lamplight came wavering to the door, and suddenly shone with a dazzling brilliance straight into the eyes of the hidden boy.

Garcias, coming forth, carried the lamp in one hand and a revolver in the other. He walked straight up to Rinky—and then turned his back upon him!

Surely he had seen! And yet, no—there he is opening the balcony window and leaning out a little.

He turned and came slowly back.

"I have to believe you, Isabella," he said. "God knows it is a bitter pain to have to watch you and suspect you. It may be that strange things will happen in the house tonight, Isabella. Close your ears. Think no thoughts. Ask no questions! Good night!"

He left the room at once, and Rinky heard the double turning of the key in the lock.

Isabella came back to him on the balcony, and beckoned him into the room.

She was rosy with excitement, and there was a sparkle of anger in her eyes.

She said: "How under the sky did you manage to keep away from his eyes? I almost fainted when he went out onto the balcony."

"He walked straight up to me," he told her, "and then turned his back on me. I was pressed back among the vines. I suppose that the leaves made a screen—and he wasn't looking for anyone to be hidden in such a shallow place."

She nodded, with a sigh of relief, and then she said: "I couldn't keep him from locking the door. You'll have to climb down again, Rinky. And heaven alone knows how you can do that. It's hard enough to climb up—let alone climbing down again."

"It's not decided, yet," said he. "Let me have a talk to the lock of that door. I may be able to change its mind."

He went to it and dropped upon one knee, and the girl came beside him.

"You can't do anything," she urged. "The key's in on the other side."

He had taken into his hand a slender, flat piece of steel, and this he inserted into the keyhole.

"It's hard," he murmured to her, "but there's a certain amount of play in an old lock—and a good deal in this one," he added.

She stood close beside him, pressing to the wall so that she could have a better view of his face.

His eyes were closed, his forehead was wrinkled, his lips were tense. He had the look of a poet composing, and a musician who interprets with all his soul.

And the small sliver of steel moved softly, slowly inside the lock. Once she heard the slightest of grating noises, and then no more. After a moment there came a light click, and the door sagged ajar a fraction of an inch.

"There it is," said Rinky, rising to his feet again. And he smiled, suddenly aware of her again.

"Now what are you going to do?" she asked.

"I have to go down."

"Where?"

"To the wine cellars, but not exactly for wine," said he.

She stepped between him and the door.

"Rinky," she said, "I know more about my father now than I even dared to guess yesterday. But I can't turn loose a pest on him, as you're likely to be!"

He merely smiled and shook his head at her.

"Whatever comes out of this," he said, "there'll be no harm for your father. I think he has a man that I want. I mean nothing but that. I want the man who's been taken from me. I may be wrong, but I've an idea that he may be here."

She drew away from the door, slowly.

"Rinky," she said, "I'll never see you again!"

"You're no prophet," he answered. "You *will* see me. Depend on it! Good night, Isabella."

"It's nearly midnight," said she. "Good morning may come in just a few minutes."

"You mean that you might leave your room and come down?" he demanded, anxiously.

"Why not?" she replied, lifting her head.

"I'll give you a good reason," said the boy, and stepping through the door, he double locked it behind him.

29

He heard the lock softly shaken behind him. He heard the murmur of her voice calling after him in angry, and yet guarded, tones.

And Rinky, listening, smiled a little. She was better than any he had known before; she was apart from all other women. And when he thought of her courage in even contemplating a descent into that house of danger, it chilled his blood and fired his mind at the same instant.

When he reached the head of the stairs, he heard a pattering of swift footfalls ascending. In an instant, he was lying prone on the floor against the wall, in the dimmest place.

Two men mounted to the second level of the house. They were booted and spurred, but the spurs did not jingle. He saw that each of them had tied rags about the boots to keep the metalwork silent.

"Suppose she should break out?" said one, in Mexican.

The other laughed softly, replying: "If she breaks out, she'll very quickly think that she's not in her father's house!" And they went on, their murmuring voices soon beyond the range of Rinky's hearing.

He gathered himself quickly to his feet again. It was plain that Garcias, not quite sure in mind about his daughter, even when a double-bolted door secured her, was placing a guard over the hall.

Ten seconds later, he would have walked out of that same door into the arms and the guns of this couple!

He passed from the stairway through an open door into the patio. A smoky lantern burned by the entrance gate, and there was a flicker of light at the dining room window.

There was a corner cracked out of a lower pane, and through this he saw three men talking earnestly together. One of them was Garcias. The other was a tall and burly fellow who wore a long cloak and a plumed hat, like a gallant of the seventeenth century. The third was a small, weazened man with the eyes and nose of a hawk, and a dense, short-cropped beard.

He seemed chiefly a listener, and a silent dissenter to everything that he heard.

"Luck runs in and out very easily with every man," Garcias was saying.

"Luck has run out, mostly, with you," said the man of the cloak.

"Well," replied Garcias, "you haven't tried your hand with him, yet."

"I shall when my turn comes," said the big fellow.

"Your turn may come," said Garcias darkly. "There may be space and time for all our turns to come, before the work is ended."

"And so I say," said the big man, "that we're fools to wait. We should go and tackle the lad where he's to be found."

"Do you know better than he?" asked the little man with the black beard, pointing toward the floor. All three followed the direction of the gesture, and then Garcias said: "No, he's bound to be right. He's never wrong!"

"He's never wrong," admitted the big man, in a grudging tone. "Only this isn't the way that I like to go about a business."

"Keep your own ways for your own business," said the little man, sharply.

The man of the cloak did not answer this remark. He merely said: "What about the dampness down there in that accursed cellar?"

"It won't rust him," said Garcias.

"But the air's bad. The lantern's burned blue down there."

"The first cellar would have been just as well. The second one, certainly, would do. But the third? I'd rather go into a dungeon that hadn't been opened for a hundred years!"

"That one has a tough skin," said the man of the beard. "Don't worry about him."

"You'll find the guard sick of his business, though," declared the big man.

"You've talked enough to make me sick of you," said the smallest of the three.

Rinky waited to hear no more.

Someone was kept in the third cellar, someone whose skin was thick, held in the bad air of the old cavity.

And it might be Slade.

The entrance to the cellars, fool that he was, he had not asked from the girl. However, it was probably in the kitchen or the pantry.

30

Inside the swinging door that led to the pantry, Rinky saw by gleams and glimmers of light several other doors.

He tried one. The moment he opened it, a smell of mustiness and stale air struck his face. He asked for no further proof that he had found what he wanted, but slipped inside, closed the door, and began to feel his way forward. Steps began almost at once.

He looked downward, not to find the way, but the sooner and more perfectly to accustom his eyes to the light.

He counted the steps with care.

There were eighteen, all deep and shallow to the bottom of the flight. This, then, opened into a wider passage, which turned and descended a second flight.

There were twelve more steps in this descent, and he judged that he was now on the first level of the basement.

Then a door slammed above and behind him. He heard footfalls coming and started running to find some doorway or turning of the passage in which he could hide.

The passage ran straight as a die before him and

then, catching his foot, he pitched forward heavily and rapped his head against the wall.

He got to his hands and knees, swaying from side to side, half stunned. When he regained his feet, he was still staggering a little, and at the same time two men rounded a corner behind him and came straight forward, carrying a lantern.

"Halt, there!" called one, in Mexican.

"Your hands up!" said the other.

And he saw the shining of the weapons they carried.

He might draw and manage to drop them both, but he was caught in a labyrinth. The sound of the firing would be heard. They would simply bottle him up in the underground damps of the house. And that would be the end of Rinky Dink!

Instead of throwing up his hands, he turned about, stood wavering a little, braced himself with one hand against the wall, and thumbed his nose at the pair.

"Who is that?" he heard one of them ask of the other.

"I don't know. I never saw him before. He's drunk," said the second.

"He's drunk," agreed the first. "A fine thing to have a drunk on our hands, a night like this!"

The lantern bearer had put down his light, the better to manage his weapons. Now he picked it up again, and the pair came on. Rinky Dink, turning, resumed a course which he purposely made more uneven than necessary.

The two came rapidly up behind him. Twice and again he was on the verge of wheeling, drawing his revolvers as he turned. But each time he controlled himself.

They caught up with him. And one was the same big fellow of the long and spreading cloak, the figure from another century.

"What are you?" he asked sharply of the boy.

Rinky turned, quickly, but with an uneven lurch.

"I'm Innocente Oñate Cambrino y Sanvaldo," said he. "And who are you? And what are you?"

The man with the cloak sneered openly at him.

"I am not drunk," he said.

"The damned red wine is the trouble," said Rinky, thickly. "It's filled with fire. And with poison, too."

"There must be a thief in it," said the smaller of the pair. "For it seems to have stolen your wits."

"My wits?" said Rinky. "Señor, I am Innocente Oñate Cam—"

"Oh, I know all of that, by this time," said the man of the cloak. "It's a long song, and one hearing of it is enough for me. What are you doing here, Cambrino?"

"He sent for me," said Rinky. "Therefore, of course, I came."

"Who sent for you?" asked the smaller man, of the beard, looking with his bright little eyes straight into the face of the boy.

Rinky assumed a cunning, stupid leer.

"You ask me for *his* name, do you? And what is yours, my friend?" he asked. "And why do you ask me for *his* name?"

"He's one of us," said the man of the cloak. "The drunken young fool!" he added, half under his breath, but loud enough for Rinky to hear.

"I'm not at all so sure," said the man of the beard. "I don't smell any liquor about him."

He moved forward. Rinky, recoiling, reached for his belt and pulled out a knife.

"I'll slice your nose for you, señor," said he. "Don't come lurching on me! We have a right to a little room, we men of the family of Cambrino y Sanvaldo!"

"Let him be," said the big man. "There's the curse of Mexico—the young bloods, the fools, the weak-wits, the empty-heads! There's nothing to be gained by talking with him."

"I'm not so sure," said the smaller and older man, still shaking his head and staring at Rinky with his little, overbright eyes.

"Why not?" asked his companion. "You can see and hear for yourself."

"Would Felipe," said the other, lowering his voice until it was hardly above a whisper, "employ such a fool as this lad seems to be?"

"He may have taken him sober, and never have seen him drunk."

"I don't like the look of this," said the man of the beard.

But he of the cloak suddenly hooked an arm through that of the smaller man, and taking possession of the situation by force, as it were, fairly dragged him past Rinky and down the corridor of the cellar, merely saying: "Let's get out of this soon. The damp will start rheumatism all through my body before long. A damned, damp piece of business, and I hope that it's soon finished."

So they went on, and Rinky, leaning against the wall, and smiling faintly, murmured to himself: "Big body, little brain; little body, great wit!"

And taking the swaying lantern as his guide, he followed it carefully, keeping at a safe distance.

It was good luck for him that he had a light to follow, for without it he would have tripped and fallen again a hundred times, so uneven was the floor in places, particularly where the naked rock was badly worn and rutted, or had been finished off carelessly in the first place.

It seemed to him that they went through twenty passages, and up and down almost as many flights of steps, and everywhere the old wine cells opened to the right and to the left with the innumerable niches where the bottles had been laid.

Here and there he passed doors, let deeply into the walls of the corridors of the cellars, and at one of these he saw his leaders pause. They seemed to fit a key into the lock, the door opened wide, and the two walked inside.

Young Grey, left in utter darkness, shut his eyes again to regain the sharpness of his vision. Then he opened them, and moved slowly ahead.

There were two doors ahead of him that he had seen, and the second was that through which the pair had disappeared.

He could hear a dim stir of voices inside; the man of the cloak was maintaining his argument.

"A poor young fool, drunk as a lord, and staggering in the hall! What could Felipe have wanted with a scoundrel like that? Well, we'll have to sweep him out of the way."

Rinky recognized the voice of the man of the beard, answering: "Rodrigo, take a man with you and go back there to the top level, and find the fool swimming in the black passages, and get him out. Tell the old woman to give him a drink of hot coffee. That may bring him partly to his wits again."

Rinky stepped back, gritting his teeth.

Wherever he moved, in this house of many curses, he seemed to flounder from one peril into another.

He thought of retreating as he had come. But no, Rodrigo and his companion would be going that way. So he hastily moved a few strides further down the hall, and coming to another entrance, he flattened himself against the door just as the other opened, and two men came out. They were dressed as vaqueros, and each was armed to the teeth.

31

From behind them, the air of the room rolled out, soiled with the fumes of cigarettes, and billowed in a mist about them. Their finery glittered through it, for they were a pair of gaily dressed fellows.

Said one who wore a crimson sash about his waist: "Señor Perez!"

"Yes?" answered the voice of the man with the cloak.

"I went in to him half an hour ago and removed the gag."

"What did he say?" called Perez.

"That the man would come for him in spite of all the devils!"

"Well," called the voice of Perez, "we are not all the devils, but a good part of them."

And to this remark there was a response of many people laughing heartily.

"I told him," said the man of the red sash, "that the other would have to be half earthworm and half ferret to come to him. But Señor Slade has a strong belief, nevertheless."

A strong belief in what, thought the boy. A belief that he, Rinky, would come to the rescue, no matter through what difficulties. And so great was that belief that, rashly, he had dared to express his confidence.

"This time his belief will do him no good," said

Perez from within. "Go on, Rodrigo. Go hunt for the young drunkard. Watch his hands, for he seems one ready to use a knife."

"If he draws one, I shall break his wrist for him first," said Rodrigo, "and afterwards his head. Come, compañero!"

So saying, he closed the door and went off down the corridor.

Rinky slipped back past the room in which the many were gathered, and now he heard, inside, the sound of a door opening, and saw a needle of light from the door chamber in which poor Slade, it appeared, was imprisoned.

He heard Perez saying: "Now, man, fill your lungs with air. It's filthy air, at best, but take a few deep breaths of it."

"I have enough as it is," answered the indubitable voice of Slade.

And the boy's heart leaped, so much it meant to Rinky, when he heard Slade's voice and knew that a single door parted him from the man who had ventured his life for the life of a stranger whose acquaintance was only one day old.

He thought back, with a warm glow, to General O'Riley, that jovial Mexican-Irishman who was able, so instantly, to put his hand upon a man of this mettle.

In the meantime, he heard the odd dialogue continuing.

Perez was saying: "If he were ten times the man

you say he is, he never could come to you. You're hopeless and helpless, here, and bound to choke like a miserable rat."

Said Slade, tersely: "Do you know me, Perez?"

"No one knows you, señor," said the other, with an odd intonation of respect in his voice. "I know a little of you, however, as you already understand."

"Have I been in many countries, Perez?"

"You have, señor," said Perez with an even more marked accent of respect.

"And have I had an opportunity to know a good many men of courage and possibilities of action?"

"There is no doubt of that," admitted Perez.

"And I have made the most of my opportunities," said Slade. "I've seen them in a great many countries, across a great many seas. But I never have seen one like this boy. He is half quicksilver and half wildcat. He is a ray of light, Perez. And he will come where you least expect him. You have a thought, now, that you are holding me securely?"

"It seems most certainly so to me," said Perez.

"And you have armed men all through the house?"

"So it has been done."

"And you have the corridors observed and men walking in them on guard?"

"Yes, that has all been done, of course," said Perez.

He seemed perfectly willing to name all his measures of precaution to his prisoner. One might have said, offhand, that there was an air of frankness, almost of friendship between them.

Perez added: "Finally, there are present four well-armed men sitting in the next room. Their ears are keen enough. And the partition between the two rooms is thin."

"I wonder," said the prisoner, "that you don't keep men sitting here in *this* room, beside me?"

"There's no need," said Perez. "Besides, the air is especially foul here, and the floor is slippery with damp. I feel, for my part, as though I already had prison fever entering my bones."

"Now listen to me," said the prisoner.

"I listen, señor," said Perez, with that same odd air of deference in his tone.

"In spite of all your precautions, in spite of all that you have done, the lad will be here before the morning. And when he comes, you will have to burn gunpowder if you wish to keep me from him."

"Very well," said Perez. "I have men who won't flinch from that."

"Be sure of them; be sure of yourself," said Slade. "I am warning you for the last time. You think that I am securely yours, but I could almost laugh."

"Very well," said Perez. "I won't argue. But if you were wise, I think that you would give up this misery and surrender this—"

"Surrender? Give up?" cried Slade. "Man, don't I know as well as you can possibly know what hangs on tonight, and the boy's search? Now get away from me and leave me alone! I cling to what I have said. I fight it out on these grounds. That's the end!"

"The end, then," said Perez.

There was a moment's pause. The boy could hear Perez muttering and cursing at something—the cords, perhaps, with which he reclosed the mouth of Slade.

And a vast pity swelled in the heart of Rinky. He could not see, looking back, what he had done to justify this man's enormous faith in him. This faith that he would pierce mountains to come to his aid. It touched him; it stirred his pride. He told himself, in that moment, that if he had a thousand lives, he would lay them all down in behalf of such a hero as that calm and strong man within the room.

The course of the thing was clear enough. They had captured Slade and striven to make him talk of the plans of the boy for the tracing of John Ray. And when he failed to speak, perhaps they had tortured him, and he had laughed at their torments, and promised them that a rescuer was even then on the way to save him. No wonder that they had been imposed upon, that they had spoken to their captive with an air of respect, and that they actually delayed the full pressure of their tortures in order to use Slade as a bait with which to capture the other.

He waited beyond the door until he heard another slammed rather heavily within. Perez, no doubt, had returned to the other room, and the light that had glinted from the keyhole was now extinguished.

Then he began to work. At the very first touch of the thin steel, he read the mind of that lock and understood its most hidden mechanism. And in another moment, he felt the sliding bolt inside it giving slowly before the pressure of the cams.

The door sagged backwards beneath his hands. Softly he let it come, for there was a slight current of air from the inside, pressing it wide. He allowed it to stand ajar, and entering, he felt his way with cautious feet and with extended hands.

It was as Perez had said. The floor was slippery and wet. The tips of his fingers, reaching downwards, touched greasy-faced mold. In the near distance, he could hear the monotonously regular dripping of water that sounded like the ticking of a clock that had run down and was about to stop forever.

So life, it well might be, was running down and about to stop for him, and for that hero who was hidden in the room, behind its thick blanket of darkness.

It was a long moment before he found what he wanted. They had stretched on the floor, it seemed, a damp, thin pallet of straw. A foul smell of decay issued from it, and upon that pallet, he felt the warm body of a man.

He felt the knees. He leaned beside the face of Slade.

"Slade," he whispered. "It is I—Grey. Thank God that I've managed to come to you. One moment, and I'll have you free."

He fumbled at the cords which held the gag.

No matter with what respect Perez had spoken to the

captive, still, he had not hesitated to bind the gag with the most cruel force upon the face of the prisoner.

How he could breathe was a wonder.

It took few seconds to loosen those cords, however. He withdrew the gag. And it seemed true that the captive had been well-nigh stifled, for his first breath, was a faint, deep groan.

It chilled the boy's blood.

He put out the knife which he carried in his left hand, and sliced the ropes that bound Slade's hands.

He swept it lower, and cut the cords that tied his feet together.

And then, as he he had feared, the door to the next chamber opened, and a broad rush of light entered the room of the prisoner, where Rinky now crouched with a revolver ready in his hand, leveled upon the form that appeared there.

32

"What's that?" asked the impatient voice of Perez from the next room.

"I thought that I heard a groan in here," said the man who appeared at the door.

He was half turned back to meet Perez's voice.

"You thought you heard the devil," said Perez. "Close the door, and keep out the moldy stink of that room. I'll be glad when this night ends!"

The man who thought that he had heard a sound hastily closed the door after this rebuff.

Rinky fell to work massaging the places where the cords had bound the ankles and wrists of the captive.

He could hear Slade panting.

"Are you better, Slade?" he murmured. "Can you stand up, now? Will you try?"

"Yes," said Slade.

"Softly, for God's sake," whispered the boy. "They're listening hard, and they have ears like foxes. Don't breathe again until we're started."

He fumbled, found Slade's armpits, and raised him to his feet.

Slade swayed, as he took the weight of his body upon his own feet.

"I knew that you'd come," he gasped, "I knew."

"No talking," whispered the boy. "You can't control your voice. You don't know how loudly you're speaking. Steady, Slade. You're not yourself!"

"I will be," said Slade.

And again his voice seemed to the boy to toll like a bell, so great was its volume!

He hurried Slade across the floor.

With one hand he helped the man forward. With the other hand, he fumbled before him, making swift strokes ahead, and to left and right. Once he slipped in the wetness of the floor and almost fell. But at last he found the door, passed through it, and turning to the left, they started up the hall of the cellar.

Only then, with what seemed nine tenths of his work accomplished, Rinky realized how great was the task which still lay before him. True, Slade

189

would probably soon become steadier on his feet as the action of walking made the blood circulate. But even if he were in the condition of a first-class fighting man, there would still be much to conquer before they were clear of the house of Garcias.

He thought of Padre José. What was the poor old man doing, now, and what was he accomplishing in his foolish task?

These were his thoughts for the first half-dozen steps, and then Slade unaccountably reeled and fell heavily forward.

The fall was alarming enough, but with it came a loud cry of surprise or pain from the crippled man.

Red rushed across the eyes of the boy. It was the end—that cry was sure to give the alarm.

He was not surprised when a door behind them was flung open, and a pale glimmer of light passed up and down the corridor. A man leaped out, and Rinky fired. He aimed low, and saw his target fall to the floor with a screech of pain.

Rinky spared him. He was no destroyer for the sheer joy of destruction. What he wanted now was to get forward toward safety.

So he turned again, and turning, he saw Slade's face, his eyes flaming, as it seemed to the boy.

"Give me a gun!" said Slade.

"Go on! Go on!" answered Rinky.

And for his part, he ran backwards. Half a dozen shots were fired blindly by hands which reached out from the edge of the door and then pulled the trigger at random, in a hope to reach a target.

He tried another shot himself, planning it so as to make a ricochet along the wall. If the bullet drove splinters of stone before it, all the better chance of striking some wrist exposed for another shot.

So he fired, and was instantly answered by a loud yell of pain and of rage. A gun fell clanging to the floor, and from the door, the half-dimmed voice of the wounded man poured forth a stream of imprecations.

That would keep those heroes cooped up, for a few seconds at the least. And now the boy took Slade beneath the arm and started hurrying him down the corridor.

He heard Slade panting: "Go on and save yourself. You've given me my start, and that's all I can ask— go on by yourself—"

"I'm with you," said Rinky, his voice quivering, "till the finish. I'm here beside you till the finish. Here's the gun you want. It shoots straight. It has six shots in it. Keep the last one for yourself, in case these devils should get their hands on you once more."

Slade made a gesture of assent.

Behind them came a fresh burst of firing. But they were around two turns from the chamber, now.

They pushed ahead into the thick blackness of the passageway, and Slade, with every moment, seemed to be surer and surer upon his feet. He was now running strongly. He seemed even more at home than the boy in the darkness.

Then, ahead of them, they saw a glimmer, and afterwards, a strong gleam of light.

"They're coming back," said Rinky. "The two that went out looking for me, likely. The noise that we make in running is covered up by the roar of the guns back there. Are the fools going to shoot at nothing forever?"

He caught the arm of Slade and slowed him to a stop.

"Here's a corner," he said. "As they come around it, hit for the head of the nearest man with your gun barrel—"

"I'll send a bullet through his ribs!" said Slade savagely.

"Dead men will do us no good," said Rinky. "But a living man might steer us through this infernal labyrinth. How far can they hear the firing now?"

"Not far," said Slade. "Not even on the cellar level above us. Solid stone swallows sound—"

Long before Rinky expected it, straight around the corner swerved the light, a lantern swinging in a man's hand. He went down that instant, from the weight of Rinky's blow. At the same moment, Rinky saw the gleam of Slade's revolver brought down with a force sufficient to crush the skull of an ox. The sudden rush of the man had apparently made him lose his direction completely, for it was the head of Rinky that the gun missed by a fraction of an inch.

Leaping to the side, Rinky jabbed the muzzle of his revolver into the stomach of the second of the two men. It was Rodrigo. He recognized the man by the broad, crimson sash that was bound so jauntily about his hips.

The other of the guards lay flat upon the floor. It would be some moments ere he rose, if ever, so heavily had the barrel of the gun rapped across his skull.

"Pick up the light, man!" urged Rinky to Slade, who stood as though paralyzed by these events. "Pick it up. Give it to this fellow. That's better!"

At the same time he was "frisking" Rodrigo, and upon the floor of the passage he dropped the two guns and the knife he found on the man.

"Now, Rodrigo—" he began.

"All the sweet saints!" breathed Rodrigo.

He was staring neither at the revolver that threatened him, nor at the man who held it, but sidewise toward Slade's bandaged head.

"Ay," said Rinky, "he's free again, and there'll be many a dead man before he's taken again. Now, Rodrigo, you've a long and happy life ahead of you if you get us out of Casa Garcias. But if you can't steer us to freedom, I'll break your spine in two with a bullet from this gun before I turn it on the others. Do you hear?"

"I hear," moaned Rodrigo. "I hear, señor. Mother of heaven!"

His moaning continued.

"Get your wits together," cautioned the boy. "Straight on, now, and go fast, but go sure. How many other men are there now in the upper cellar?"

"No more, señor. I've just been through it."

"And in the level above?"

"At the farther end—"

"And can't you go up the nearer way?"

"Yes. There are broken stairs—we could try it."

"Go on," said Rinky. "And you after him, Slade. I'll be last. You have a gun. Shoot him through the small of the back if he tries to dodge away. No, never mind that. You carry the lantern, and I'll tend to the shooting. Go on, boys! We're two-thirds of the way to the clean open air again!"

So they started on, running in single file, with the lantern dancing crazily in the hand of Slade.

Twisting through the winding galleries, they came to a door through which they passed into a small room, and out of this arose the broken stairs of which the Mexican had spoken. Half of the steps were missing, but it was easily climbable. Up they went, toward the top cellar floor.

They had come to the second winding, and all noise from beneath them had died out completely, when they saw a strong glare of light and heard voices immediately above them. At the head of their means of exit was a room of some sort, and in that room there were lights, and men posted to guard the way!

33

The three halted upon the stairs.

Rodrigo leaned on the stairs toward Slade and Rinky.

"Señors—amigos!" said he. "You see what we have done? We have come up a blind alley. There is no passing, here! We must turn back!"

But, as he spoke, it seemed that a door opened beneath them, and a burst of shouting voices, very dim with distance and with intervening walls, came with a tremor to their ears.

"You hear that?" said the boy. "We go on. There's no turning back. Straight on, Rodrigo. Slade, jab your gun into the small of his back. Put out the lantern, we don't need to hold a light for others to shoot us by!"

The lantern was accordingly extinguished.

"Up, up!" Rinky whispered. "They're half blind with their own talk, now. Straight up, Rodrigo, if you want to live. Straight up, Slade, and we'll run through them before they know that we're near. No shooting. We'll trust to our heels."

At the same time, there was, as it appeared, another door opened beneath them, and the dull, ominous roar of many voices shouted together far closer to them than before.

This uproar was plainly audible in the room above them, and as they stole ahead, they heard the wrangling end.

Said Garcias' voice: "What is that? Name of God, what is that thing I hear?"

"The wind," said the third man.

"The wind? It's the whole of the devils raised by that fiend of a gringo of whom they have told us! He is here, and he is fighting with our men. Up, up, and down the stairs, here, to help them—"

It was Diego, a big, rawboned, powerful man, who now suddenly appeared in the doorway immediately in front of Rodrigo. He carried a short shotgun in his hands, whereas Rodrigo was unarmed, of course. But the latter's fear of the shotgun was far more than balanced by the pressure of the gun on the small of his back, it appeared.

He swayed forward as Diego stepped into the opening, and with all his force he smote the big man in the stomach.

Surprise probably hurt unlucky Diego more than the fist. He doubled up, however, and fell backwards, the shotgun hurtling out of his hands.

And over his body the three ran.

Rinky, coming last of the three, saw in the corner of a small room—half littered with old boxes and barrels—a small man with the face of a fox, bending over a cask and gripping the edges of it as though he wished to lift it and hurl it. But Rinky knew the staring eyes and the white face. The man was frozen to stone with astonishment and with fear.

But close to him was a fellow of a different caliber, for Garcias now was whipping out a long-barreled

196

revolver, and bringing it calmly down to a level for a shot. He was none of the fancy gunmen, the snap-shots. He apparently believed in slowness and surety. And Rinky feared such a fighter more than a dozen of the more flashy sort.

But he himself was one of those oddities who can combine speed and accuracy. His Colt was already in his hand. He took a cross shot at fat Garcias, aiming, as always, low. He tried to strike below the hips. He had no will to seriously harm this valiant fat man.

And he saw Garcias sway and stagger, then bring his revolver down and fire!

It was poor Rodrigo who swayed sidewise like a tree chopped through by the axes of the woodsmen. He threw out his arms and fell on his face. That man was dead, or nearly dead, said young Rinky to him-self, and he gave Garcias the compliment of a second bullet that brought him down out of sight behind the cask.

Before them opened the narrow mouth of a doorway that yawned upon a stairs beyond.

Rinky scooped the lantern from the top of the cask, and hurried on behind Slade.

But he found Slade like a man bewildered, standing still, his revolver poised in his hand, a des-perate look glinting like sparks from his eyes.

He seemed to be staring at Rinky himself, like a man about to shoot!

The boy caught his hand at the wrist.

"On, on, Slade!" he gasped. "Get up the stairs. We

have two parts of a chance, after all of this!"

And Slade, as though recalled to himself, turned and fled up the steps, with the boy behind them.

They reached a higher level. It was that of the kitchen cellar through which Rinky already had passed, and here he was able to guide, calling to Slade, as the latter ran ahead of him, the various turns which ought to be made.

They got to the last steps, mounted to the pantry, and cast the door wide.

How many minutes before had Rinky gone down through that same doorway?

Hours—centuries? Only scant minutes, but here he was returning, with the prize he sought before him.

Always before. He caught Slade by a heavily mus-cled shoulder and steered him as a man steers a boat through crowded waters. They blundered together into the smoky light of the kitchen, through the rear yard, and so came out beyond a fence of young saplings.

In this manner they stood, at last, under the tall, looming, black wall of the house, and still, like a miracle, all of the house beneath them was still. Not a sound, not a breath, not a whisper came from the tumult which must be raging in the bowels of the house.

What would happen?

Who was the "he" of whom all of those hardy fel-lows stood in such awe, from whom they took their orders, for whose disapprobation they seemed ready to die rather than to merit?

These thoughts came to the boy.

But, at the same time, holding Slade close by the arm, he was steering him forward to the spot where the mule had been left.

He took the revolver from Slade's hand, saying, "You'll travel lighter and faster now. And speed is what you need. Speed, speed, speed! Run, Slade, run. The devils will all be ranging for us, soon!"

At that moment, to tag his words, a wild uproar broke from the house. And then a score of shots in rapid succession.

But Slade and the boy were already in the thicket and there they fairly stumbled over the mule, lying peacefully asleep.

34

Isabella Garcias, when she was left alone in her room by the departure of Rinky Grey, swept a shawl around her shoulders, since the night was turning chilly, and sat down on a couch in the dimmest end of her apartment. She was brooding bitterly on the very name she bore, and telling herself that of all things in the world, she would the most readily part with the name of Garcias.

She had grown up in the old house and learned at first to have a certain affection for the place. She had loved Garcias himself, also, in the beginning, as a child will naturally turn to a real or imputed father. But then she learned the gruesome story of Fernando and his brother, and that hunting "accident"; and after that, she could not tell whether Fernando Garcias really loved her as a daughter, or whether her adoption into his family had been a sort of act of penance to make his peace with God for the greatest of all sins.

Now, as she sat in her room, Garcias' big house seemed to Isabella a vast dungeon.

She heard the deep murmur of two men speaking quietly together just outside her door.

They had been posted to make sure that she remained inside!

When she realized this, an angry frenzy came over the girl. She jumped up from the couch and began to walk hastily up and down the room.

Where was Rinky Grey?

Why were the men in the house?

Then her mind concentrated on the remembered picture of the boy kneeling at the door, working at it with the sliver of steel.

Then she remembered, in the room, a lariat with which she often had practiced, on foot and on horseback, when as a youngster she had envied the accomplishments of the vaqueros. It was not full length. It was hardly more than thirty feet. But the supple rawhide was still quite strong, no doubt.

When the idea came to her, she instantly had it in process of execution. She brought the long coil, tied an end of it to the strongest pillar of the balcony, and at once she went over the side.

She had not gone down three arms' lengths before she realized that, like a headlong fool, she had not taken care to measure the distance to the ground, and see how close the rope reached to it. Furthermore, her strength was not sufficient to climb up the rope again. And as for the wall, the rope hung out more than a yard from it, and she could not reach its crevices!

She was suspended in midair, and a scream came up to her lips and made them tremble. But she checked it and forced the sound back in her throat, half choking.

Then she resumed the descent. She gripped at the rope with her knees, but it was too narrow for her to gain much hold in this manner. Then she came to the last handhold of the rope and found that her feet still swung idly above the ground.

How far could it be?

She turned her head and looked, but because of darkness and dizziness, she could see nothing but what seemed a limitless well of black.

It was useless to scream for help, now. Calmly she told herself that, even if by a lucky chance her voice were instantly heard inside the house, she could not maintain her hold on the rope until help came to her, and a ladder was brought.

She closed her eyes, and threw back her head.

If only the fall would be long, and the death mercifully sudden!

She relaxed her hold, and dropped down into space. Her knees buckled; she fell flat; and lying there, looking up at the glorious brightness of the stars which she had never expected to see again, she began to laugh. There as she hung at arm's length from the rope end, she had been practically standing on the ground!

She began to circle the outer limit of the walls. When she came opposite to the entrance to the patio, she made a wide detour, to the verge of the brush, and coming back on the farther side, she went down the row of the windows, doubly black, in that they were on the northern side of the house. Not even the horizon stars cast their images into the panes of the glass.

She came, in this manner, to that same hall in which young Grey, not so very long before, had seen Perez and the man of the beard talking, but it was a different pair that she saw within, now.

It was her foster father and old Father Joseph!

35

She was amazed to see Father Joseph.

The shepherd was now filling his pipe out of a red, cloth sack. He lighted it. Midway in this operation, Garcias broke out: "Any night but tonight, padre, I would be happy to see you here. I know that you are a great friend to Isabella. But tonight I have important things to occupy me."

"I understand the nature of your business tonight, Señor Garcias," said the priest.

Garcias was so struck that he remained agape.

"Now, Padre José," he said, assuming a tone of lightness which it was clear was not natural, "you have a very keen wit, but I don't think that you can have looked into the midst of my business tonight."

"We all feel," said Father Joseph, in his gentle way, "that there are veils that fall over us, as if from heaven, shutting us off from the view of other men. Ordinary, common men, we call them to ourselves. For each one of us possesses a unique radiance, from his own point of view. Well, señor, I sympathize with your attitude. But still you may be wrong. Perhaps I have peeked through the mist into your most secret thoughts."

He smiled as he spoke.

"Perhaps, perhaps," said Garcias, impatiently looking over his shoulder toward the door—a very broad hint to his guest. "But now, Father Joseph, suppose that you tell me what's in my mind at this very moment?"

"Murder," said the shepherd, without emphasis.

The word lifted Garcias half from his chair.

"Murder?" he echoed. "You don't often make jests, Father Joseph."

"Murder is in your mind," repeated the old man. "That is why I came here tonight."

Garcias forced out a ghastly laugh.

"Murder?" said he. "Then tell me who it is that I wish to murder?"

"The young American who has stayed with me, with his hurt friend," said the padre.

Garcias bit his lip. He was turning gray, as a man does when all his body is immersed in icy water.

"I am to kill the young American," nodded Garcias, beginning to sneer. "And why should I wish to kill the boy? I have seen him."

"So he told me," said the shepherd.

"He told you, did he? And the little jest we played on him?"

"He told me of the little jest, too," said the shepherd. "This has been a lucky day for you, señor. You already have been closer to death than the thickness of a spider's thread. And still you are sitting here, and able to speak words."

Not the slightest passion had crept into his voice.

"You tell me that I wish to commit murder," said Garcias, "and you tell me that the man I am to murder is the young American. But you haven't told me what makes you so sure."

"Because," said Padre José, "you stole away the other American from my hut so that the boy would follow you back here."

"So? So?" said Garcias, his face more frozen than ever. "Padre José, you are a fellow of a great imagination."

Then he added: "Since you know these things so well, as it seems, tell me then my motive in wishing to destroy a young man I have never seen until this day?"

"Your motive?" said the shepherd. "Oh, your motive comes from outside. You were asked to do the thing, and promised a great deal of money for the doing of it. You are to murder him, so that he may not find John Ray."

"May not find John Ray?" cried the other. "May not find a dead man? What nonsense are you talking, José?"

"Not dead, though he has been missing," said the shepherd.

"Ah?" said Garcias. "If you know so very much, José, no doubt you are sure that the man is alive?"

"Yes, I am sure," said the shepherd.

Garcias actually writhed in his chair with excitement.

"You have even seen his face, I dare say?" said Garcias.

"Yes. Every week or so I see him."

"You know even where he lives?" cried Garcias.

"Why should I not?" said the shepherd. "I know his house fully as well as I know my own."

"By heavens!" muttered Garcias. Then he asked: "You wish me to believe what you say, José?"

"Oh, I think you will believe me," said the shepherd. "Because the truth is that you cannot think I would lie to you, now that I've come so close to the end of my days."

"José," said Garcias, "if you know so much as this, I still cannot think that you would come and tell it to me, if you also believe that I have in mind the purpose which you attribute to me."

"And why not?" asked the shepherd.

"No one but a madman would speak as you have spoken," said Garcias, "if what you believe of me is true."

"If you could see your own face, my son," said the shepherd, "you would understand how clearly the guilt is written on it. God forgive you for it as freely as I could forgive you."

Garcias groaned aloud in excitement, in shame, and in anger.

"Make this clear to me," he said. "What earthly thing would you gain by coming in this manner?"

"I gain the life of the boy," said the old man.

"What is that to you?" asked Garcias sharply.

"I have known him one day, and I love him," said the old man.

"You love a thief, then, and a man-killer!" said Garcias spitefully.

"I love a brave man, and a truthteller," answered the shepherd.

"Tell me, after all, how what you say is of service to him?"

"Why not? Suppose that you trap him and destroy him with your hired men, still you have accomplished nothing. For if he does not come back to my hut in the morning, then I shall send word of the truth to John Ray."

"What truth will you tell him?"

"That a rich man is fighting away death until he can hear of John Ray, and if Ray is living, he will be made the heir to six millions."

Garcias leaned back in his chair, stunned.

But as he sat there, a fire gathered gradually in his eyes.

"If we suppose that everything you say is true," said he, "then you are a rash fellow."

"In coming here?"

"Yes."

"No, not a rash man, because you believe me, and you will not kill the boy for nothing. No matter how your trap is set, you know that it will cost your people some of their best blood to deal with him. You will be glad to let him go when you understand that I, after all, am the only person in the world who knows where John Ray is to be found."

"And if you are brushed out of the way, Padre José," said Garcias, "then there would remain not a single soul who could find Ray! That is clear!"

"I am in no danger," said the shepherd. "You are not a man of many scruples, Señor Garcias, but still even your hand would be held by a small thread from destroying me. Partly on account of Isabella, and partly on account, let me be vain and say it, of myself."

"And if I have other men?" questioned Garcias, who seemed fascinated by the course of the argument.

"They are almost without exception the men of the mountains. And the men of the mountains have a certain respect for me, and even a certain fear. They would be more apt to help me, if I asked them for help, than to serve you, in spite of the money you offer to them. Think a moment, and you will see that this is true. However, if God takes me, he takes me, and that is an end of everything on this earth, for me. I should not be very sorry. I have traveled so much of the way that I think I know what the rest of the road is like."

"You are a brave man, and a good man," said Garcias. "I admire you. I respect you. But, as you have said, there is one man above me, in all this. I must ask *him* what to do. I won't say that all of your guesses have been wrong. Wait here. I shall return, soon."

"Thank you. There is no hurry," said the padre.

And Garcias left the room. The girl, listening with all her might, thought that she heard the key turned in the lock.

Apparently old José heard the same thing, for he instantly left his chair, crossed to the door, and tried the knob of it. It turned in his hand, but the door did not budge.

And José, turning slowly from the door, clasped one hand upon his breast, frowning at the floor.

Isabella walked stealthily down the side of the patio, came to the floor of the hall, and was amazed to see the key in the lock. By so small an omission of care, her guilty foster father might be saved from the crowning crime of all.

She turned it, the bolt moved back, and she thrust the door wide.

Padre José was seated in the chair, calmly smoking his pipe, and he turned his head only gradually toward her.

Clinging to the side of the door, weak with relief

and joy, she cried feebly to him: "Come, padre! The way is clear, as you see! Come quickly, quickly!"

He leaned forward to rise, and she glanced swiftly over her shoulder to make sure that there was still no one in sight.

When she looked back at the padre again, he had not left his place!

"Padre José!" she cried in a sudden terror. "Are you coming?"

"No, my child," said he.

36

She could not believe what she heard.

She cried at him, more loudly still: "Padre José! Do you hear me? The door is open!"

He shook his head, as in resignation.

"Go away quickly, my dear," he said to her, "or you will be seen here. As for me, I have made up my mind, and it is not so easy to do that. Nothing matters to me, now."

"Padre José!" she cried. "You are quite mad! He will have you murdered."

"Oh, Isabella," said the shepherd, "murder or illness or old age or honorable battle, they all bring one to the same end. But it is different with you!"

She sprang inside and closed the door behind her.

"Isabella!" he exclaimed.

"I am staying here, if you do," said she. "I'll be a witness."

"Child, child," said the shepherd. "You are only his daughter in name, and not in blood! You cannot tell what he would do in such a case."

"I'm not his daughter in name or blood after tonight," she answered. "But I stay here so long as you stay. I'll go when you go."

He went hastily to her and took her hand.

"Do you mean this?" he said.

"Yes, I mean it," she answered.

"Now, God teach me what to do," said the good old man. "I must stay here for the boy. And yet I should go to take you, Isabella, if you really are leaving this house."

"Forever and ever," she answered, passionately. "And now every minute that you wait here is dangerous to you! And besides—"

Now, swelling louder from the bottom and the rear of the house, they heard the sound of many voices shouting, and then the booming of guns, firing rapidly.

"Whatever has happened, it's finished now!" cried the girl.

"The poor lad!" cried the shepherd. "And no soul to help him. It is he. It could be no other person! Let me go, Isabella—"

He tried to run toward the noise, but when he had gone as far as the door, she clung desperately to him.

"If they've killed him," said the girl, "do you want to kill his work after him? You know John Ray."

"Curse the name of him," said the shepherd, fiercely. "Except for him, there would be none of this crime and this wretchedness! But you are right. If he is gone, then I must save myself to do the thing that he has left undone. If I had told him before—if only I had told him before—"

So, half groaning, he turned at last to the girl, and with her hurried out of the patio.

Behind them, the uproar now increased to a great volume. And a voice that yelped above the rest came to their ears.

"That is my father," said the girl. "No, he is only Fernando Garcias to me now. He is mad with rage. He has failed, and I swear that the young American is living. Living and free or there would not be this uproar. He is shouting like a frantic man."

"This way," said the shepherd. "If this is true, then God has been good to me! This way—there is a mule left yonder in the woods—"

They hurried on. Presently, as they reached the trees, they saw just before them the shadowy silhouette of a mounted man. The girl, with a gasp, caught at the arm of her companion and strove to draw him back, but he merely murmured to her: "Whoever it is, he is likely to be a man who knows me."

He called aloud: "Who is there?"

"Someone who has been waiting for you, Father Joseph," answered a voice. "You're a little late, partner. What's all the fireworks yonder at the Casa Garcias?"

"It is he!" said the shepherd. "He is here again. It is the boy, once more."

Isabella said nothing at all, but her hand shook upon the arm of her companion.

They hurried on.

"Who's with you?" asked the voice of Rinky, again.

"Isabella Garcias," said the shepherd. "Or Isabella of some other name tonight, for she's thrown away the last one. Who is that beside you on the other horse?"

"It is Señor Slade," said the boy.

"You have done the thing you wanted to do," said the shepherd. "This is a night of miracles."

"Wait here with them," said Rinky. "There's a whole nest of horses back in the woods, where the thugs staked them out. We'll take what we want and give the others a run before us. Garcias and his pets may not follow us so fast then!"

They did not wait. They pushed on behind him, and they found in a small clearing at least a dozen saddled mules and horses. On a mule they mounted the girl, and put the shepherd on another. The reins of the others were cut rapidly, and as brush crackled under the feet of men who were rapidly approaching, they started the herd before them, and swept down into the trail to the lower valley.

Shouts and curses followed them. Even a few random bullets went crackling through the branches not far from their heads. But they got safely onto the trail, and rode steadily away.

The thin moon, riding higher in the sky, gave them a very indifferent light, but their mounts were used to mountain trails, and they went forward at a good rate.

Slade led the way, his shoulders bulking broad and heavy before the rest, the girl followed, the padre behind her, and last of all rode young Rinky, with a song continually bubbling softly on his lips.

"Ask Padre José, Rinky, what news he could have given to you long ago," said the girl suddenly.

"What news, father?" asked the boy.

"News that would have ended your trail, Rinky," urged the girl. "For he knows where John Ray lives!"

"*He* knows?" broke out Slade, with a hard, high ring in his voice.

"You have a right to be angry," said the shepherd. "I should have told you, as soon as I knew what was keeping the pair of you in the mountains, where there was so much danger for you both. For failing to do so, I nearly brought ruin to you both. I intended to tell you, also. But you must remember that it was not an easy thing for me to say. For fifteen years, John Ray has lived true to a promise to himself that he would never tell the world again his name. Fifteen years of truth to such a course of life is not an easy thing to violate."

"Of course not," said the boy. "But tell me now, Father Joseph. All that I want to do is to find the man. If he's near, I'll start now on the trail for him. Give me half a hint of the way to ride, and I'll start now. Eh, Slade?"

"Start now?" said Slade, the same ring in his voice. "Yes. Even if we had to ride over ice and fly down cliffs. What is it, Father Joseph?"

"A thing you will find hard to believe," said the old man.

"Hard to believe?" said Slade. "After tonight, there's nothing in the world that's hard to believe. I have seen a dozen armed men behind locked doors fail to keep out one youngster who had made up his mind to enter. After that, Father Joseph, what is there in the world that would be hard to believe?"

"Stuff!" said Rinky, modestly, but happily.

"It's truth," said Isabella. "It was a glorious and wonderful thing. You haven't told us a syllable of how you did it!"

"I'll tell you the whole story," said the boy. "I started walking, and I had good luck beside me all the way. Besides, that's ended, but John Ray isn't. Padre José, suppose that you tell us now where the trail to John Ray lies."

"Come, come," said the shepherd. "You are all fire and eagerness. Do you know the story of the boy and the wishing gate?"

"Oh, confound stories," said Rinky, impetuously. "Tell me where I can find the way to John Ray?"

"You want to cut me short," said the old man. "But I won't have you clip the wings of my story, because it's a reasonably long one, and strange enough to be worth the telling, I think."

37

Rinky groaned with impatience, but the shepherd, like one who loves words, cleared his throat and imperturbably began: "We go back to the last days of John Ray in San Vicente. All of you know a good deal about him? Yes, for I've heard you all speak of him many times. He was the sort of a fellow who catches the eye, not that there was very much to him, but the worst sort of a fool can turn himself into a light if he soaks his clothes in oil and then touches a match to himself.

"That was the way with John Ray. He had made a good deal of money. He had made so much of it that he thought he had enough to last forever. He got tired of taking gold out of the ground, you might say. And he decided that he would use the rest of his life to spend the coin he had piled up.

"So he settled down in San Vicente, because it was pretty, pleasant, and he already knew it well. Besides, he wanted to be the center of attention, you see, and therefore he chose a comparatively small place. He was like Caesar in this. If one may compare such small things with great ones.

"When he came to San Vicente, he had so much money that he felt he could buy the whole city, if he chose, and keep it or throw it away. Perhaps for that reason he took a great affection for it, and for the people in it.

"You know those people in San Vicente are cheerful, good-natured, and nearly all of them are pleasant to talk to. When they saw what sort of a fellow had come among them, they very quickly gave one another the wink, as the saying is. They agreed with each other about him. They humored him to his bent. And he was happy.

"Why, the happiness of that man, if you could have seen him in those days, was a shining thing that could be seen at a distance. He was a great fool!

"But all he would know was what his eyes saw and what his ears heard.

"If he went into a theater, there was an outbreak of hand-clapping. When he went down the street, men and boys took off their hats to him.

"Why not? It is an easy thing to salute a fool or a madman. Such people are humored, like children.

"If he was riding by the river, people stood up on benches, and looked, and clapped their hands, and laughed. He thought that they were laughing in sheer pleasure at the sight of him. He did not guess that there was any mockery in them.

"In a short time, he loved all the people of San Vicente even more, in his heart, than they seemed to love him in their manner.

"It followed, since he was rich, that the beggars of San Vicente began to come to one door, only.

"Well, that was a good thing, too. He liked it. He used to set up a big round table in his gardens and around that table the mendicants gathered. Sometimes there were thirty or forty men and women out there. In the field behind his garden, he set up some tents. Those beggars lived in a sort of gypsy camp. They had plenty to eat, red wine or pulque to drink, and in addition, tobacco was distributed among them. That's enough to make a Mexican happy, and they were very happy. Nothing pleased John Ray more than this gypsy camp, and he felt as if all of those lives were in the hollow of his hand.

"At any rate, the years ran merrily along for Ray. And every year it seemed to him that he had worked his way deeper into the hearts of the people of San Vicente.

"One day, he heard a pair of youngsters talking loudly, and one of them swore 'by the beard of Señor Ray. By the double beard of the señor!'

"That filled Ray's cup. Poor idiot! Poor, childish idiot. He felt that he was almost deified in the eyes of the townsmen, and after that, he turned on the tap of his fortune and let it run, and filled the very gutters with it, so to speak.

"But a running faucet will drain the biggest tank, in time. Suddenly, Ray wakened with a note from his bank.

"He had a few thousand pesos left, and that was all.

"Well, he looked at the letter and shrugged his shoulders.

"It was true that he had not invested his money in banks or in farms or in stocks. But he had done better. He had given it to honest and honorable people.

"So he simply went to a great friend of his, a man who dined with him every Saturday of the year, and he said to him that he now had need of a part of the two hundred thousand pesos which, from time to time, he had loaned the fellow.

"He was greeted with a silence.

"And when he looked at his friend, he saw that the face of the man was pinched and distorted with fear and with greed. He said that, at the moment, he was without ready cash, but that he would soon raise the money, and if John Ray would come three days later, at three in the afternoon—

"John Ray came three days later, having spent his last penny in the meanwhile. And when he came to the door of his friend, he was told, coldly enough, that the man was not at home. And the servants did not know where he was. Or when he would return!

"Even to John Ray, this thing was now clear. He said good-by to two hundred thousand pesos which he had given without asking for interest, note, or security.

"He went to another friend; it was the same story.

"Suddenly a number of people left San Vicente. They were all friends of John Ray. They were all people who owed him quantities of money.

"And he understood, at last. It was not that he had loaned money to one rascal, but that the whole list of his friends had turned against him.

"One evening, as he sat in his room with both his hands hard-gripped on the table before him, a note was brought to him, it was from General O'Riley. The general never had received a penny of benefit from Ray, but in the note he said that he heard hard times had come to Ray, and he declared that the American was a public benefactor, and said many other pleasant things, and begged John Ray to use his checkbook as his own. And, with that note, he sent a little sheaf of checks which were not filled out except for the big, sprawling signature of the general.

"When Ray saw this note and looked at the contents, something crumbled in his brain, as though his wits were dissolving in a flame. He threw the note and the checks into the fire. He ran down to the stable and saddled his best horse, and he rode out into the open.

"He rode through the streets of San Vicente, and cursed them as he galloped. He rode under the cypresses by the river, and cursed them, also. He galloped on. He crossed the bridge. He saw a road before him.

"He hardly knew where it went. He only knew that there was an open way before him, with green, naked fields on either side, and no men—no men! For that he was grateful.

"He rode far into the night. He rode until the horse reeled beneath him, and fell down dead. He looked at its glazed eyes and at the white foam around its mouth, and he felt no pity.

"He walked on, and still he only knew that he was

walking away from San Vicente, and the face of man. That was his only goal, do you see?

"He got into the mountains at dawn, and there half a dozen vagrant ruffians met him, stripped him of everything, threw him some of their rags, and went off.

"He put on the clothes, and he laughed.

"For he felt, suddenly, the stripping away of a great burden.

"Do you understand how it was with him?

"After his life of wealth and struggle and happiness, and heartburning pain, in the end he was as he had come from his mother's womb—naked and helpless, except for his two hands.

"He stood on a high place and looked back, and saw the sun redden, and the green plain of San Vicente, and the white of the town, and the river running like gold through the plain.

"It was a little thing, do you see? He could have held that distant town in the hollow of his hand.

"And so he laughed again, and the last bitterness washed out of his heart.

"I want you to understand. He had been spending his time, his money, to make San Vicente a thing that he could hold as his own, through the love that the people had for him. But now, as he left the town far behind him, he saw that it was worth nothing. It was the beginning of understanding for him.

"He said to himself: 'John Ray has lived, and John Ray is dead. I shall forget him as quickly as the world does!'

"He stopped at the house of a charcoal burner and got a razor and shaved off his beard.

"Then he went on and came through a pass into a narrow valley, and he found a sick old shepherd sitting on a rock, with his head hanging, like the head of an old horse that stands in a corral and waits for death.

"So John Ray began to work for the old man, and that same winter, death carried the shepherd away, and John Ray, with a new name, inherited the flock, and kept on living among the mountains, as you see him to this day!"

When he had finished, a wild, sharp cry burst from the throat of Slade.

"*You* are John Ray!" he cried. "You, you! Oh, eternal fool that I am—and already I had half guessed—half—"

He broke off, with a click of his teeth.

But young Rinky had reached out and grasped both the hands of the shepherd.

"You see what's happened, Father Joseph?" he said. "The thing you thought that you'd thrown away has come back to you, and now you're to be richer than ever!"

38

In this brief narration of a life and the tragedy within it, it seemed to Rinky that he had beheld a thing greater than the great mountains around him.

He heard the old man saying: "Have I told you the whole story for nothing, my son? Do you think that I wish to be John Ray, of San Vicente, or New York, or Rome again? No, no! Money can buy me nothing, now. Nothing remains that I value except the peace which I find inside the arms of the mountains. These simple people, they truly love me, and they need me. They come to see me as if I were a father, a judge, and a priest. Could all the millions which Forbes leaves to me accomplish so much? No, that money would gather around me liars and sycophants, again."

"True!" said Slade, suddenly and with force.

"Listen to me," said the boy. "Do you think that your life will be safe? We know the truth about you. Slade—I don't know how—already had guessed it. Garcias, and the other scoundrels, may guess it also. Your life will not be long, if you stay here!"

"As for my life," said the old man, "it was a gift for which I did not ask. And it will be taken away from me as such gifts are always taken. Do you wish me to run away, like a frightened dog? No, no, my son. I remain here."

"Father José! Father José!" said Isabella. "Don't

you see, you're just as blind and stubborn now, in a different way, as you were in San Vicente?"

"Well," said he, "perhaps I am. We see only by what light is within us, and that is only a feeble glimmer to shine down a very great road, my dear."

"You've looked at it," said the boy, "from one side only. If you look at it from another, you'll see something that's worth seeing. You'll see that there's that poor fellow Forbes, yonder in a sick bed, fighting away death for four years, setting his teeth, living on milk and water, praying and waiting for news of you, Father Joseph. Now, are those four years to be thrown away like a bad penny?"

"Ah, ah," said John Ray. "That's a thing, too. I should have thought of that. Poor Forbes on his sick bed, and four years of waiting—four years of pain and expectancy! Why, I can remember eating my heart out because a train was half an hour late."

He added: "You see, my children, what a fickle and changeable old man I am! I shall do as you say. Not to take the money he wants to give me, but to see him, and thank him, and perhaps to give him something that will make the end of his days pleasant—that's why I shall go to see Forbes. Ay! But I shrink when I think of the distance. Besides, what's to become of my sheep?"

"True," said the girl. "There are the sheep!"

But she laughed as she spoke.

They had come, now, within sight of the round-topped hut of John Ray, and they were surprised to see a light gleaming from the open doorway.

But John Ray said: "That is simply one of my people. Some one has come for me, and will sit there by my lantern until I come back. That often happens. They will miss me, I think, when I have gone on the long journey!"

He said it with a simple happiness, and Rinky, looking back into his memory, thought of the picture of the man with the divided beard, galloping fiercely under the cypresses.

This was not he. This was a new man, in a new life, with another soul.

39

As they came up to the house, no one stepped out from it. They dismounted, and Slade held the horses while the girl and Rinky went in with the old man.

There arose from a stool to face them a tall, long-nosed, freckle-faced man of about forty, dressed in a flannel shirt several sizes too big for him and a coat that hung upon him in folds.

He looked at the shepherd, and then he turned to Rinky.

"Why, Rinky Dink!" said he. "Doggone your socks, but I'm mighty glad to rest my eyes on you. I've come a long way to parley with you, son!"

Rinky shook the big, bony hand of the other, explaining to John Ray: "This is Jim Parson. Jim is an old friend of mine. We've punched each other on the nose and got up friends. You know what that means."

"But you got up the soonest," said Jim Parson, "and I got up the most friends. Ay, man, but I'm glad to see you now, you will-o'-the-wisp, you burn-by-night. I've rode myself sore to get to you!"

"What is it?" asked Rinky.

"Why," said Jim, "I've traveled all the way down from the border, son, and I come from Neilan."

"Does Neilan want a report?" asked the boy.

"He wants to send you a warning, that's all. He's got a new word. Do these people parley English, son?"

"As well as you do, Jim."

Jim Parson drew the boy to one side.

But his voice, harsh and hoarse as it was, was louder than he meant to make it.

"The marshal has a new tip, Rinky," said he.

"About what?"

"About the game that you're riding on. And he got the name of a man that may put the kibosh on you."

"Where did he get that?"

"Why," said Parson, "he got it from Broom that's just turned up, after being given up for dead."

"Ah, I'm glad of that!" said Rinky. "But Broom is a tough one and he would take a lot of killing."

"He got almost enough to do the job for him," said Parson. "That's what he got! But he lived through, and come to El Paso a pretty skinny shadow of the Broom that we used to know. Cast-iron, we used to call him, eh?"

"That's right," said the boy. "What about him?"

"I tell you what I seen. I seen Broom setting in a chair, among friends, talk about things that made him bust out crying."

"I don't believe it," said Rinky, compressing his lips.

"Nor would I, if another man told me," answered Parson. "But I tell you what I seen, and the shame was so clean gone out of him that he never even cared about his tears, but he sat there and blubbered like he was two years old. Oh, he was hurt bad, was Broom. He was hurt to the quick and the quill of him, man!"

"I hate to hear it," said Rinky. "What happened to him, poor devil?"

"What happened to him? That's what I'm here to tell you, and who done it."

"But how did you find me, old son?"

"I found your trail. It was a hard job. I hit a fellow called O'Riley that gave me a steer in San Vicente. And out of that, I made out something. And I did a lot of talking in bad Spanish now and then, and so I got here, at last!"

"Poor Broom," said the boy. "I would have bet on him against a thousand."

"Ay, but he met one man in ten thousand, and it was him that put Broom down."

"One man?"

"Ay."

"Mexican?"

"American."

"What was his name?"

"His name was—"

A revolver shot boomed in their ears, and poor Parson spun like a top and fell his ungainly length to the floor, both arms flung out wide.

Rinky let him fall. Instead of catching that lumbering weight, he conjured two revolvers into his hands, and whirling toward the door, he faced—Slade!

"Slade!" he gasped. "Slade—in the name of God!"

"In the name of the devil!" said Slade, calmly.

"This is a thing that you'll have to answer for," said Rinky.

"To whom?" asked Slade, as calmly as before.

"To me. I'm a friend of his and an older friend than I am of yours. I've owed you something, Slade. But I've owed as much to Parson. What's got into you, man? What's wrong with you?"

"I said that I'd get them, one by one," said Slade, in the same manner as before. "I swore that I'd get them, if I had to live a thousand years to do it. And here's the first one. This is one of the devils that I found in Garcias' house!"

"You?" exclaimed the boy. "You found *him* there?" He gaped at Slade.

"He's the one," said Slade, "who wanted to polish me off here and not wait to get you. But then the other had the bright thought of using me as a bait to catch you, and Parson agreed. Why, it was Parson that swore the best place to put me, as a bait, was in the third cellar, because he said that the deeper they put me, the harder you'd try to find me. Parson is the one, lad. And thank God I've paid him off!"

"Jim Parson," said Rinky, blanching. "Old Jim! Why, we've been hand in glove. We've bunked together. I can't believe it of him!"

"It's a hard thing," said Slade. "But money rots the soul of a man!"

"Yes," said the voice of John Ray, who, with the girl, was kneeling at the side of the fallen man. "Money rots the soul of the world!"

"He's not dead," exclaimed Isabella. "Thank heavens for that."

"Not dead?" exclaimed Slade, with a ringing lift to his voice. "Not dead? With a bullet through the middle of his brain?"

"It glanced!" exclaimed Isabella. "There—see the frightful furrow that it made down the side of his skull! He's living, and I can feel his heartbeat. Don't you, father?"

John Ray was pressing his ear to the breast of the fallen man.

Said Rinky: "It's a bad business, Slade. I've had enemies. I've had men that I hated and hunted, even, but I gave them their chance when it came to the final showdown. I don't shoot men when they're not looking, Slade!"

"You've lived only a short time down here, Rinky," said Slade, in his even way. "But let me see. You say that he's not dead, yet?"

There was something about that last word that made Rinky watchful, and started his flesh crawling.

He saw Slade step across the hut to where Parson lay, and with a sudden movement, Slade brought a revolver into his hand.

It would have been far too late had not the boy been on the alert. As it was, he was barely able to leap and catch the hand that held the gun.

He found himself contesting with an iron arm, but a little trick that he had learned from an old Japanese in California helped him, and he made the gun fall out of the numbed fingers of Slade.

He growled at the man: "Slade, you've gone mad! You're losing your wits. What the devil's inside of you?"

He found himself facing eyes that glared at him with a straight, fiery regard.

If the boy could have believed what he saw, he would have said that there was hate in the look which the other gave him.

Then, without heed for the gun which lay on the floor of the hut, Slade turned on his heel and left the place.

Rinky, his brain spinning, followed to the door of the house, and was further amazed to see Slade spring upon the back of a mule and gallop down the road.

Slade was gone, but where?

To cool himself off, perhaps.

"Nerves," said Rinky to himself. "He's had more than he could digest at Garcias' house. Poor Slade!

He's had a good deal. It's touched his brain a little—and no wonder!"

Yes, Slade had been through enough to turn the mind of even such a man as he!

And yet, the pity of it! For Rinky had begun to look upon him as a matchless hero, a man with nerves of steel.

Rinky turned back, as Parson groaned on the floor, then gasped, and finally sat upright.

He presented a strange appearance, with blood trickling down over his face in three separate streams.

He clapped a hand to his head and said: "That's the way with 'em. The body's the proper place, but they *will* try for the head. Who was it, Rinky? Who did it? And what did you do to him?"

Rinky could not answer. It seemed impossible for him to face his old friend and say that he had done nothing to apprehend the would-be assassin.

And then a thought struck him like a thunderclap. It made him stagger. It was a thing not to be believed, but it forced him down upon his knees beside the wounded man. He caught Parson by the shoulders and shook him a little, regardless of his wound.

"Tell me, Jim," he said. "The fellow who broke Broom's heart, who was it?"

"Him?" said Jim Parson, rather dreamily. "Oh, yes, I remember, now. That's what Neilan wanted me to tell you. Him that smashed Broom. Him that's killed others that traveled your trail—a fellow by name of Slade—"

40

Upon the ear of the boy, the name fell like a pistol shot.

He heard the confused exclamations and the astonished words of the girl and old John Ray like the babbling of running water in the distance.

He looked back upon the words and actions of his guide. Now that the blow had fallen, all seemed clear enough. It was Slade's own ingenious mind which had devised the plan for luring him to the house of Garcias. When the boy left the house that day, Slade must have wandered up the valley and given warning to Garcias and the brigand to make the first attack upon Rinky, which had so nearly succeeded. And then Slade it was who made of himself a living bait to bring on Rinky to a sure destruction.

The part seemed so utterly detestable that the boy could hardly believe it, at first. And this from a man who had risked his life for him?

Yet he could remember, now, that at the inn, on that other night, the door had been mysteriously opened, as if from the inside, and Slade had made no motion to assist him until the attack on him had definitely failed, and the man in the hall had been put to rout.

Was it not Slade who had suggested the lighting of the lamp, thereby having his companion hold the very light by which he was to be shot? Only the accidental failure of the first match had saved Rinky even as early in the game as that!

And yet he groaned when he thought of the trust he had placed in this man. It had seemed to him that Slade stood out among other men as the crowning peak stands out above the range. Then that rush down the hall in pursuit of the scoundrel who had lain in wait was the merest sham, for all the while Slade knew that, barehanded though he was, he was in no danger from the brigand! The accident of the fall upon the steps was what had completed and made the performance perfect!

Again, the boy could remember in Garcias' house that night how Perez had talked to the captive. No wonder he had been troubled about the gag, and the cords, and the plan. For it was the master of them all who was lying there bound, at his own order!

How completely Slade had seen through him, in planning that last, contemptible coup!

But what other signs there had been in Garcias' house, such as the fall of Slade in the hall, and the blow he struck with the revolver that barely missed Rinky's skull, and the moment when he had turned upon him at the top of the passage—murder had been in the heart of Slade all the while.

Yet it seemed strange that he had not given the alarm at other times—for instance, when Rinky had just cut the cords, and the door from the guardroom had opened upon them. True, it had been the groan of Slade that caused the door to be opened but one syllable, after it was wide, would have caused the armed men to rush in.

Perhaps, no matter what a villain, something in him was stirring in response to the situation. He had told them with his own tongue that, in spite of dangers, Rinky would reach him. Perhaps now a grim pride in the accuracy of his prediction may have made him silent at that crucial moment. Besides, he must surely have been convinced that the game was still in the hollow of his hand, even when he saw them stealing up the corridors, with Rodrigo to guide them.

And yet, when Rinky looked up from his reflections, having completed in his mind the train of evidence which proved that Jim Parson had spoken honest words, his face was sad.

The girl saw it. She was helping old John Ray to bandage Parson's wounded head, but she had time for one smile of sympathy and understanding.

"He's not worth your sorrow, Rinky," said she.

Rinky went outside and stood under the stars, trying to think.

Slade and Garcias and all their hired men grew dimmer in his thoughts, now. He was thinking of John Ray, and of that dying man, Forbes, and of the need of bringing them together.

He was thinking of that man with the battered face, yonder in the northern city, Marshal Neilan, who at his desk had planned all this.

In honesty there is strength, and well do the honest

men know it, but the thieves and the scoundrels know it better still. Otherwise, how could Neilan have done so much?

He was not as intelligent and subtle of mind as Slade. He could not have conceived the deep schemes of the latter. But nevertheless he was multiplied in his strength by the power of right.

Never before had the thing appeared to Rinky so manifest. His heart warmed. He only hoped that when Marshal Neilan knew what his emissary had done, he would approve all.

But the work was only half done.

He had found John Ray, which none of the others had done. And now he had the second half of the task to perform—to escort John Ray north to the land of stronger law. Perhaps to usher him to the bedside of Forbes.

A full half of the task that lay unfinished still before him. And Slade and Slade's money and men were all against him.

But the right was with him; the right stood on his side; and he felt, somehow, that he could lean upon that abstraction more than upon any of the party with him.

For what a party it was! An old man, a young girl, a badly wounded man—and himself. Not a party to help him, but three separate weights upon his powers!

"Now, then, Rinky," said the voice of John Ray from the doorway, "what do you think the best thing to do?"

"San Vicente," said the boy. "That place first, where General O'Riley will surely help us all he can—and that all is a good deal. And with his help, then north as fast as we can ride—or else down to the sea and take a ship—"

"There's a sad trouble with O'Riley," said John Ray. "It is that he cannot help telling all that he knows. And in his house there are always servants who are ready to pick up the news and spread it. He has no more real privacy than a horse in an open pasture."

The boy was silent. He could not help feeling the truth of these remarks.

"For another thing," said Ray, "the moment that you get inside of San Vicente, even if you only stay a few hours, you are sure to be marked, and the life of every one of us is in danger."

"The lonelier we can stay," put in Jim Parson, "until we hit the Rio Grande, I reckon the better it will be for all of us."

"I know these mountains," said Ray. "I could guide you through them blindfold. We have livestock to carry us. I know the way. And it seems to me that the best thing is to break through and head straight across the northern desert for the Rio Grande. It means a long ride and a hard ride. But I would lay my money that the last thing your friend Slade suspects is that we'll go north, instead of turning east toward San Vicente. Mind you, it's the San Vicente road that he'll have his hirelings watching now. If we can gain a quarter of a day's march on him by starting now—perhaps we'll beat him to the finish."

"Where is the girl to be left?" asked Jim Parson.

He said not a word of the pain of his hurt. He had made and was lighting a cigarette as calmly as though the bandages were not now strongly gripping his torn scalp.

"Where is the girl to be left?" repeated Rinky.

And both of them faced John Ray.

At this, Isabella threw up her head.

"The girl does not need to be dropped. You can ride on, and she'll take care of herself."

"Would you go with us?" asked old Ray, turning to her.

"No," said she. "I wouldn't go with you. I wouldn't weight you down."

"If she stays here," said Ray, "Garcias will have her again. He knows his rights as a—father! And now that the mask is dropped and she's seen him as he is and he knows that he has been seen, you'll lead a sweet life, my dear. It won't be long till he's married you off to a fat fortune, frijoles and grease and all!"

"I can take care of myself," said Isabella.

"Listen to me," said Ray. "She can shoot much straighter than I. She can ride much better, and much longer, and she's lighter in the saddle. She must go with us!"

"I'll not be bullied and bandied about," said she.

"Come, come," said Rinky. "It's time that we took you in hand. Father Joseph, you finish talking to her. We'll get the horses ready for the march."

41

They were ten days to the north, now, and they had had no sign of an enemy on all that march. Confidence grew up in them. They made their fires fearlessly at night and in the morning, regardless of how far the smoke column might be seen, or the bright eye of the fire glance through the darkness.

And all through that march, the girl held up bravely and steadily. She made no complaints. She refused no hazards. And when she dismounted at a halt, she was the readiest hand to collect forage, or cut down brush for the fire.

She would be the last to turn into her blankets, and the first to rise in the pink of dawn.

And all day long the men looked at Isabella as though she were the music and the dance of running water.

For three days Jim Parson, who bitterly opposed the inclusion of her in the party, looked at her sourly. On the fourth he went to her and said in the hearing of them all: "I been a fool, and a great fool. Look you here, Isabella. You're a better man than I am, a better hand around a camp, you ride slicker, and you got more sense."

Out of the mountains, four days through the sands they rode, and the work was harder than ever before. But still there was no token of an enemy at hand.

The heat had increased every moment, after

leaving the high lands, and since there was now a full moon shining at night, they started their marches not long before sunset, and pressed on through the cooler hours.

Their guide was no longer old John Ray. They had long ago passed north of his domain and, crossing a no-man's land of which none of them had much knowledge, they now reached a region over which Rinky Dink had ranged many and many a time.

So he guided them at last into a narrow pass that cut through a low-lying range of rocks. Beyond those hills of stone, it would not be long before they had the long, brown sweep of the Rio Grande before them.

The night was utterly still as they entered the pass, and from the rocks of its narrowing walls and from the sands under their feet, the heat was still pouring forth. The place was an oven which had not yet cooled.

Only Isabella Garcias seemed cool and at ease.

They had nicknamed her The Salamander, because heat seemed to make so little difference to her. And now, as they rode along in a scattered single file, she was singing, from time to time, and whistling like a boy.

Rinky rode behind her. And now old John Ray urged his mule up beside the mare.

"Rinky," said Father Joseph, "for five miles you've seen neither the sand, nor the rocks, nor the moon in the sky. You've looked at nothing but the girl."

"Father Joseph," said the boy, "for fifty years and fifty thousand miles, I could ride along and look at nothing else."

"Have you told her that?" asked Father Joseph.

The boy looked sharply askance at the other.

"Tell her that?" he said. "She knows it. She knows the way I feel. There's no need of talking. And she knows, besides, what I am. She knows that I'm a loafer and a drifter and an idler. Those are the kindest things that you can call me, in fact! No, no, Padre José—the less I talk to her the better."

"Well," said the old man, "if you don't talk to her, I shall talk for you."

"Hold on," said the boy. "You wouldn't do that! You don't mean that, padre?"

"Why," said the other, "I'm fond of the girl, am I not, my lad?"

"Of course you are."

"And suppose that a person I'm fond of has a gold mine on his farm and doesn't know anything about it—well, what sort of a friend would I be, Rinky, if I said not a word?"

Before Rinky could answer, the sand splashed before his horse, as water splashes when a stone is shied into it. Jim Parson and the girl, in the lead, looked suddenly back to them, and at the same time, from the black rock wall of the ravine, to their right, came a sound as though two hammer heads had been struck together.

The four, in silence, stared at one another. No

words were needed. They had underrated Slade, after all, and now he was at them.

"Back, back!" called Rinky. "Turn back and—"

As he spoke, he whirled the mare about.

Instantly, the sands splashed to the right, to the left, and ahead of them. Deceived by the clearness of the moonlight, the marksmen on the walls of the ravine must have fired pointblank. But they would soon make the necessary allowance for distance and then that fire would tell.

Jim Parson sang out: "They've got the place lined for us. We've gone and shoved our heads into a trap, Rinky. Make for the rocks, straight ahead. That's better than—damnation—this!"

All in a troop they spurred their mounts for the rocks which jutted up in a black, jagged group not far from them.

The girl, being in the lead and a light rider, gained on the rest; but the white furrows were leaping in the sands about her as the marksmen increased their fire from either side of the ravine.

Then Isabella's mustang stumbled and turned head over heels. She herself lay in a crumpled heap just ahead, a dark spot on the white of the sands.

Every man of them would have given his life for her; but it was the good sense of Rinky's mare that brought him first to her. He leaned from the saddle as she strove to sit up, and drawing her up before him on the saddle bow, he rode on into the shelter of their little fort.

240

She was their first concern, but she dismissed their worries, instantly, leaping down from the saddle to the ground.

To be sure, she staggered a little, but with one hand leaning against a jagged stone, she recovered herself and managed to speak a word to Rinky.

"Poor horse!" she said. "And poor all of us, for I think that he is only one jump ahead of us on the long trail."

42

It was the first discouraged word that she had spoken, but there was reason for her discouragement, now. The rocks which had seemed so safe a retreat, from a little distance, were found to be a most open nest. On every hand there were gaps among the big stones, and through these the marksmen on the ravine walls were firing blindly, hoping to strike a target.

So first they made the horses lie down, and then they sheltered themselves at the bases of the biggest rocks. Then, in the hot stillness, broken only by the clang of the rifles, and the splashing of lead against the outer walls, they had time to consider.

They might live through one day, without water, the sun beating straight down upon their heads. But the livestock would perhaps go crazy or die before that day was ended. And after that? They could pray in vain for a cloudy night in this place, in any season of the year. And without clouds, this moon beat upon the valley like a silver sun.

No, hope was as dim and distant for them as ever it had been for Rinky Grey on that night of nights when he wandered through the damp, vast cellars of Garcias' house. It was more distant, even, for there he had had the advantage of darkness to aid him and cover him, and twisting passages through which he could dodge as a fugitive.

But here all was light. All things that threw a shadow were mercilessly visible from the rim rocks of the ravine. Beside the dead mustang lay a small image of darkness. Though the body itself, even at the small distance from the rocks of their refuge, was almost invisible, still the shadow stood out to a distance.

Rinky stretched himself. His feet, instead of slipping easily through the softness of the sand, struck into the resistance of Jim Parson's slicker which lay there—the old gray slicker, turned by the moon into the very color of the sand.

He picked it up and looked hopelessly out through a rift between the two rocks opposite him. It was almost the last move of young Rinky, for a rifle bullet clipped a lock from his forehead.

Another man would have cowered back into shelter; Rinky merely crouched like a cat ready to spring. Some shrink from a blow, others leap at the striker.

And suddenly his mind was perfectly clear. He saw

their future as though it were mapped by his own hand. Either this night something must be done to save them, while still they possessed their full strength, or else they were totally and miserably lost.

"Hello!" said Jim Parson. "There's a fellow riding out across the sands toward us. He's waving something as he comes."

"A flag of truce, eh?" said Father José. "Let him come up."

The rider came within ten yards before he halted. The moon cast a steep black shadow across his face, but the voice that came from him was that of Garcias.

"Isabella?" he called.

She stood up among the rocks.

"I am here," said she.

"Ah, child," said Garcias, "I thank God when I see you and hear you. I have begged on my knees, and he has permitted me to come for you. The others are lost men, but men they are, and they will let you come out to me!"

"Ay, Isabella," said Father Joseph. "Go out to him. Better Garcias than what is coming to the rest of us!"

She turned her head, deliberately looked at Padre José, and then turned back to her foster father.

"Father," said she, "for all the kindness you've shown me, I'll pray for you and wish you well all the days of my life. But to go back to you—I'd rather go back to red hell!"

"You speak, child," said he, "because of that one

night. You can never know under what impulsion I was placed, or how I struggled against it. But the truth is that I was not my own master, and all that I did was only for the hope of pushing your own fortunes forward. There was nothing for myself!"

"Do you think," she answered, "that murder would have helped me? Not the first murder, either! Oh, Fernando Garcias," she added with an outbreak of emotion, and a sort of childish wail in her voice, "I loved you as though we were the same blood. But that night I threw away the name you gave me."

"Ah, good girl!" said Jim Parson, through his teeth.

"Isabella—" began her foster father again.

"Listen to me, you hound!" said Jim Parson. "The girl's spoken the truth. It's a better thing for her to take a bad chance with us than a worse chance with you. Turn your hoss around, or I'll knock out your teeth with a half-inch slug of lead. I've got you covered now!"

That ended, abruptly, Garcias' mission. They saw him ride off, striking his hand against his face. They heard his groaning voice. And then the pitch of it rising to curses which died out, at length.

And there was a murmur as the people within the rocks began to confer again. Father José was outraged by the manner in which Jim Parson had cut off the girl's chances. She herself was firm that her old life was ended, and that she would rather die than go back to it. And Jim Parson vowed that if she were his dearest sister he would rather shoot her through the head than allow her to return to such a man as this.

"And what do you say, Rinky?" asked Father José, turning about from the talk.

But Rinky was not there!

"He's gone!" cried Isabella. "He's gone to try some wild, crazy, hopeless thing. I should have watched him. I meant to. I knew beforehand that he would try! Rinky! Rinky!"

Anxiously they scanned the sands, from all sides of the rocks, but not one of them caught sight of Rinky Grey.

A long hour and more passed, and then, at the rim of the valley, where a small gorge opened from it and a trickle of water ran down, to be soaked up in the sands of the larger canon, something seemed to rise out of the desert, and take on the shape of a man.

It was Rinky, and what he rose from was not the sands themselves, but Jim Parson's old slicker, gray battered, and filled with wrinkles, the color of the sand beneath the moon.

Under it he had crawled on hands and knees, slowly, slowly, like a turtle.

And once a bullet struck the sand just before him.

He had lain flat, and waited for the second shot to break his back, but no second shot came. Someone had thought he saw something move across the sands, no doubt, and had changed his mind afterwards.

So Rinky came to the verge of the rocks, and then, among them, safe from observation, he stood up, with a fire in his eyes that was no reflection of the moonlight.

He had fought fair, even against thieves and liars and traitors, but now he would fight for the sake of the girl who was yonder crouching among the rocks. And God help the man who got in his way!

He rounded the corner of the rocks, and saw the smaller gorge before him, the southern half in blackest shadow, and the northern wall gleaming with light.

Two men walked among the rocks, close to him, and he made himself small as they passed by him.

The voice of one was Garcias', and the voice of the other was Slade's. Garcias led a horse. Slade was without one, and walked with a jaunty step, swinging a stick.

The boy heard Slade saying, "Make the round. Tell every man that his pay is doubled the minute the job is done, and a good bonus besides. As for the girl, Garcias, women don't matter really. They're appurtenances and properties of a man's life, not a vital part of it. She has to go. She has to go with the others. It must be a clean sweep. I tell you, the boy has turned her head. She's seen him playing the part of a hero. She can't help but be in love with him, and after his death, you couldn't keep her from blabbing."

He waved his hand again. The air of the man was jovial, bursting with confidence.

"Tell every man that the time when he must keep

his eyes open, specially, is about the time of dawn, when there's just enough daylight to make the moon dim. That's the hour when they may try to make a rush. If the rush is made, let them train every shot on the boy. For once he's down, the others are nothing—dust in the fingers—that's all. Garcias, the game is won, the greatest game I've ever played. The cards are in our hands. We only need common sense and open eyes to push the thing through to the end."

Garcias, without an answer, his head bowed a little, rode away. And Slade, looking after him, threw back his head and laughed silently, as a wolf laughs when it sees the calf stray within its reach. So Slade laughed, and then, turning a little, he sauntered up the bank of the twisting stream, swinging his stick, like one who has finished, or almost finished, a great task, and now gives himself a little relaxation.

Now Rinky straightened from the rocks, and stepped out after Slade. He walked in time with the other, but with a slightly longer step which quickly closed the distance between them.

He was very close when he called out: "Slade!"

Slade did not turn. He stopped short, frozen in the midst of a step, and Rinky saw the man shudder from head to foot.

"Slade," said Rinky. "I'm going to kill you. I've fought before. But I've never fought for the sake of killing. You're different. You're not human. Still, I won't do as you tried to do with me. I won't take you from behind and murder you. I'll give you a fighting half chance. You can turn, and fill your hand as you turn. Because the moment you're around, you're as good as dead. And as you die, Slade, I want you to know that your scheme has dissolved in smoke. It's disappeared. It dies with you, because the rest of the rats will run when they smell your dead flesh down the wind. And if—"

He was watching, as he spoke, and it was well that he did so, for Slade chose that moment to whirl, a gun in his hand.

It seemed to Rinky that for his own part he never in his life had drawn a gun with such deliberation, and never aimed so calmly and with such a cold surety. And yet his bullet was in Slade's brain before the latter had pulled the trigger.

43

He left Slade lying by the verge of the creek, with his face upturned, smiling toward the starry sky, and his eyes open and as brilliant as they had been in life. His right hand lay in the water, as though with his final gesture he strove to wash it clean of sin.

"Slade!" called a voice. "Slade!"

And a tall Mexican came hurrying with great strides. Rinky drew back among the rocks.

"Slade!" yelled the man again. "Who fired up here—"

He saw the dead man, then. He came close with his hands stretched out before him, as though he were thrusting away the thing which his eyes saw. But when he came up to it, he whipped suddenly about and ran back in the direction from which he had come. The moon was on his face, and Rinky never had seen such incredulous horror as he saw there. There was the fitting tribute to Slade—that the ruffians he had employed could not believe in his destruction, and were utterly unnerved by it when it came.

From the mouth of the smaller ravine, hoofbeats began. Rinky followed to the corner where the two valleys met, and he saw the fugitive streaking across the distant sands toward the south as though pursued.

So it happened. Exactly as he had imagined, exactly as he had told Slade himself, the death of the leader dissolved all the work which he had done, and the last and surest of his traps faded into smoke, and was lost in the pink of the morning mist.

They were gone. The very last of them was gone!

And so he walked up to the little natural fort, smoking a cigarette, and waved to them. And big Jim Parson, with a wild whoop, started to run out to him, and then flung up his hands and jumped back behind the rocks.

"It's all right, everyone," said Rinky, drawing close. "We're as free as the air. There's nothing but miles between us and the Rio Grande, now."

They did not swarm about him with outcries and questions. They came out slowly, like animals from a den, and with hollow, weary eyes they looked at him. Only the girl, last of all to come, held back close to the rocks. Her eyes were reddened and swollen as if with weeping. She looked at him as at a ghost, and not a true man.

"Rinky, man," said Jim Parson, at last. "Will you tell us what happened?"

"Why, they simply blew away like dust," said Rinky. "Slade died during the night. And the rest of them took to their heels."

"I ain't a man that loves questions," said Jim Parson, "neither puttin' nor takin' 'em. But how did you fade yourself into thin air, last night? And how did you get at Slade in his crowd?"

"You know, Jim," said the boy. "I just had a streak of luck."

It was not really charlatanism, but because he could not put his tongue to the words. To explain it would be too simple. But in his own heart he felt that there *was* a mystery in the thing, and that from the time he received Marshal Neilan's commission, he had been acting under a guidance which he did not understand.

So it was that there grew up in the legend of Rinky Grey, or Don Diablo, the ghostly tale which was rumored and whispered from town to town, and from camp to lonely camp. Three sane and safe-witted people attested the fact of it. And who could offer an explanation? To this day some of the old-timers will sit with pencil and paper, drawing the diagram of the valley, and offering their explanations of how Rinky crossed the sands. But no one hits upon the simple truth. No one ever connected the death of Slade with the odd fact that a certain slicker, under the moon, appeared the very color of the sand.

They saddled their horses and mules in haste. All offered their mounts to the girl, but she declared that she had earned the right to walk as well as the best of them. Rinky fixed a baleful stare upon the other two. It was old John Ray who accepted the hint, and pulling Parson by the arm, made him ride on. Rinky watched them go, and when they were a little distance away, he spoke to the girl as she started after them.

"Isabella," said he, "I'm a mighty tired man. But if it comes to a showdown, I'm going to put you into the saddle."

She turned about, staring at him.

"Rinky," said she, "if I thought you were really foolish enough to lay a hand—"

"Stuff," said he, and with a laugh of confidence he strode up to her.

Now his first step was long and strong, and his second slipped a little in the sand, and his third was very short indeed. And at last he stood still. He wanted to keep his eyes on her, but he found the task a hard one.

His glance was slipping away.

"Suppose that I give it up," he said, "and simply beg you to take the mare, and let me walk along beside you. We'll change places, after a while. But

251

you know, Isabella, I feel like walking alongside and looking up—like one of those squirrels!"

That was how Isabella came to take the saddle on the bay mare. But somehow they did not seem able to overtake the other two riders very easily, though surely the mare could outstep the mules.

John Ray and Jim Parson took turns in glancing covertly back, and each time one looked the other asked: "Well?"

And he who had looked would answer: "Nothing—yet!"

Until at last Jim Parson, as he glanced behind, suddenly reined in his horse.

"It's all right, Padre José," said he. "You can turn around and look now. The whole world can look, and they won't give a damn. Now, there's a pair of high-grade folks. But look at 'em makin' a show of themselves. Look, now, will you! They're walkin' along hand in hand, like any fools. Maybe Rinky Grey won't continue to win all his battles to the end of his days."

Some six weeks later, Marshal Neilan came wearily home to his house. The day had been a long one, and the marshal was even a more tired man than usual. But as he passed through his front gate and a shadow detached itself from the hedge, he turned like a cat, and a gun jumped into his hand.

"It's all right, marshal," said the voice of Rinky Grey.

"Rinky, confound you," said the marshal, with a breath of relief, "when will you get over your ways of a hunting cat? Why do you have to wait for me in the dusk, when you've a right to prance down the main streets in the middle of the day? Are you still afraid?"

"You know, marshal," said the boy, "habit's a pretty powerful thing."

"Ay," said the marshal, "it is. The eating habit, for instance. Come in and have supper with me."

"Thanks," said the boy, "but the fact is that she expects me—Isabella, I mean—"

"Oh, let her wait and expect," said the marshal.

"Let *her* wait?" murmured Rinky. "No, sir, I know better than that."

"Well," said the marshal, "here's another letter from John Ray. He's coming West again. He's bound down there to Mexico. He only wants to stop off for the wedding."

"Is Forbes dead, at last?" asked the boy.

"Dead? There's the trick of it. It did Forbes a lot of good to see Ray. It did him so much good that in a week he was sitting up. And in another week, he started walking. And he's put on ten pounds and says he'll live forever. It wasn't heart trouble. It was a fool doctor's fool medicine. Digitalis, or something, when no digitalis was wanted. And so it looks, son, as though you've had all your work for nothing, except for putting Forbes on his feet."

"Speaking of work," said Rinky, who did not seem

to heed the rest of the marshal's speech, "it seems that Isabella thinks that I ought to have some sort of a job. D'you think that you could find me one?"

"D'you know cattle?" asked the marshal.

"No."

"D'you know sheep?"

"No."

"Can you run a farm?"

"My God, marshal," said Rinky, "what are you talking about?"

"I'm talking about work," said Neilan. "What sort of work can you do? You don't seem to be much good!"

"I know it," sighed Rinky. "That's the way it seems to me, too."

"You could do my work," said Neilan, "for next to nothing a year and good chance to get yourself filled with lead once a week."

"Neilan," said the boy, "why didn't I think of it before! I take the job right now!"

"Better ask Isabella, first," said the marshal.

"Ay," sighed Rinky. "I suppose I had."

Center Point Publishing
600 Brooks Road • PO Box 1
Thorndike ME 04986-0001 USA

(207) 568-3717

US & Canada:
1 800 929-9108
www.centerpointlargeprint.com